WAITING FOR THE LAIRD

LOST LOVE
BOOK ONE

WILLA BLAIR

OLIVERHEBERBOOKS

HIGHLAND SEER: "…this is different enough from other Highland romances to stand out from the pack. Ms. Blair's writing style is natural and evocative…"

— ROMANTIC HISTORICAL REVIEWS

HIGHLAND TROTH: "...trickling danger and suspense in perfect amounts...Scottish romance at its best!"

— IND'TALE MAGAZINE

WHEN HIGHLAND LIGHTNING STRIKES: "Ms. Blair is a consummate storyteller…Can't wait for more from this magical author."

— MY BOOK ADDICTION AND MORE

HIS HIGHLAND ROSE: "Another awesome Scottish Romance!"

— MY BOOK ADDICTION AND MORE

HIS HIGHLAND HEART: "The plot was honestly a masterpiece. It was well thought out and orchestrated. Right out the gate I was hooked! The hero had immediate book boyfriend appeal."

— LONG AND SHORT REVIEWS

HIS HIGHLAND LOVE: "Fiery passion burns bright in HIS HIGHLAND LOVE! Readers who enjoy Highland romance should definitely try Willa Blair's books."

— BOOKS & BENCHES

HIS HIGHLAND BRIDE: "Ms. Blair has delivered a wonderful and captivating read in this book where the chemistry between this couple was strong; the romance hot..."

— BOOK MAGIC, UNDER A SPELL WITH
EVERY PAGE

And for Author Willa Blair: "I thoroughly enjoy Blair's work and recommend her Scottish love stories to all!"

— ELIZA KNIGHT, USA TODAY BESTSELLING
AUTHOR

To everyone who has ever lost a love.
May you find another where you least expect it.

"*I*f I don't see some sunshine soon, I'm going to pack up the twins and move back to California!" Lara MacLaren gazed out the window of the tea shop, then back at her friend Becky, who frowned at her as if she'd lost her mind. Well, maybe she had. The past year had been rough. Now the days were noticeably shorter, and what little sun there should have been was hiding behind thick clouds, scuttling the emotional progress she'd made over the summer. God, she missed California sunshine.

"Why on earth would you want to do that?" Becky demanded before taking a tiny bite of her oatcake and venison entrée, then patted her mouth with her napkin. "Sunshine is so ordinary there. Ours is rare and beautiful. Surely you must prefer our sort."

Lara snorted at her put-on aristocratic English accent. Becky did part-time clerical work for the estate agent who handled the purchase of Cairn Dubh for Lara and her husband, Angus. Her sense of humor had appealed to Lara, and the two had become occasional lunch and shopping-expedition buddies in the months before Angus's passing.

Since then, Lara had been too exhausted by grief and focused on her nine-year-old twins' needs to spend much time with her friend, though Becky had tried several times to get her out. A few days ago, she'd invited Lara to meet on Friday for lunch in the village, to get away from the renovation mess at Cairn Dubh. Lara's improving appetite had convinced her to accept. The timing was perfect since workmen were breaking through a stone wall today into the old north wing. She was happy to get away from the noise and dust for a few hours.

Lara couldn't spoil her first social occasion by spending the entire meal complaining about what had happened to her family. She wasn't sure how to answer Becky's question without whining, but she had to try.

"After Angus's funeral, I thought about staying in California," she admitted, determined to make light of it. "Even talked to my parents about moving in with them for a while." She rolled her eyes. "Now there was a truly bad idea…"

"No doubt," Becky answered in typical droll Scottish fashion.

Holding up a hand, Lara continued, "In my defense, I worried that the unfinished parts of the house, which was most of it back then, weren't safe for Amy and Alexander. And Scotland is a very long way from my family and friends."

"So what brought ye back? I've always wondered. You lived here only, what, six months, before…"

"Angus died." Lara shrugged off the hollow in her belly those two words always brought on. "Yes, I can say it." She glanced at the ring on her left hand and sighed. "He died really young. Of a stroke, of all things. In California, on a business trip." She pursed her lips, then added, "Being able to hold his service there was convenient for our families, certainly." She managed not to roll her eyes. "I'm not sure he would have chosen to be buried there once he moved us here, but there he remains." She crossed her arms, kicking herself for opening the door to this conversation. She was fidgeting, but Becky seemed not to notice.

"But not you and the twins," her friend prompted.

Though reluctant, Lara supposed now was as good a time as any to get some of the last year off her chest. Becky's gaze was warm, concerned and comforting, as if she really wanted to know. Lara had avoided sharing the details for months, and Becky had to be curious.

"I suppose the reason is that I'd come to love the house, the area, and," she paused and smiled at Becky, "the people. I'm not sure how it happened, but Angus's vision became mine, too. I couldn't bear to leave any part of Cairn Dubh in ruins. Every time I considered staying in California, something drew me back to Scotland and to making Angus's dream come true." She shook her head and glanced out the window at the clouds. "It doesn't make sense, I know." It would make even less sense to Becky if she knew how rocky the start of their marriage had been. Or perhaps not, given what they'd overcome.

Becky reached across the small table and squeezed her hand, pulling Lara's gaze back to her.

"I'm glad you chose to stay," she said with a lift to her lips. Her smile widened as she let go of Lara's hand and leaned back. "It took you some time, but you've found a good man to finish the restoration. The work is well underway. By spring, it should be done, and everything will look brighter." Becky cast a narrow glance at the lowering sky outside. "I can't wait for that, either."

Lara thought back over the past year while she traced circles on the white tablecloth. Despite her best intentions, she'd found everything about the project too heavy a weight to carry alone. Being the general contractor was Angus's area of expertise, not hers. Once she accepted she had too much to learn to be effective, she knew what she had to do. In early June, she had finally gone through the paperwork Angus accumulated during his search for a general contractor, though he'd eventually decided to run the renovation himself.

"Did you know Ian has almost no online presence?" Before she'd decided on architect Ian Paterson, she'd searched the web for information about the contractors Angus had considered, to round out what she learned in Angus's files. "He's got a business website with lots of information about past restorations. Before and after photos and glowing reviews from previous clients, but not much about him, other than what he needs to establish his qualifications."

Elsewhere online, she found the same bare-bones education and work history he'd provided on the resume in Angus's files, and little else. Ian did not have a social media presence—not that she could find. "I felt like a stalker and hated prying…"

"It was necessary. Best you know who you're dealing with," Becky reassured her.

"Well, clearly, the man spends very little time online. Does he live in this century, or is he lost in the past with the buildings he restores?"

Becky laughed at that.

Lara couldn't help but join in, then she sobered. "He won't say much about himself, even now. But he won me over when he said he could imagine how hard it must be for me and the twins to live with Angus's dream unfinished."

"Ach, lass…that sounds just like him."

Though she was committed—and Ian had a contract—Lara was glad to hear her intuition about him confirmed. He might have been the only architect to call her back and meet with her, but something about him appealed to her, so she'd hired him on the spot. He'd spent the past four months completing the last two rooms Angus started in the main part of the house and its upstairs guest rooms. He'd also finished the south wing, where the family bedrooms were, which had been built shortly after the main house. He took the work seriously and made sure the craftsmen he hired did, too. "I believe I made a good decision, yes." Lara finished her tea and set the cup aside. "With his help, I'm making progress on what Angus and I started together…" Her throat closed suddenly, and she couldn't go on.

Becky nodded in sympathy and finished the sentence for her. "...To make a home out of an old ruin."

~

"There he is again!"

Peals of childish laughter echoed through the halls of Lara MacLaren's Scottish manor house, Cairn Dubh, punctuating the cadence of running feet.

Since getting home from school, Amy and Alex had been whispering about "it" when they thought she couldn't hear. When they knew she could overhear them, they used their twin-speak, a verbal shorthand that made them nearly unintelligible, even when they were standing right in front of her. It drove her batty, but their closeness also warmed her. She supposed keeping secrets from her was one of the ways they comforted each other since their father suddenly passed away.

If only she had a twin to comfort her.

But, of course, she did—two of them—when they weren't driving her to distraction.

"Be careful, you two!" Lara didn't know what set them off this time, but the unseasonably warm weather in the Highlands had recently turned to cold and snow. With Halloween approaching, it would be easy to imagine ghosts and goblins in a centuries-old place like this. Most likely, a mouse had taken up residence. The stray cat that had moved in with the cold weather probably chased the mouse into its hole with the twins in hot pursuit.

The lovely warm fire in the hearth made it hard to leave

the library, but she knew her twins. She set aside her book and shrugged on a sweater. Past the dining room and kitchen, the "hallway to nowhere" that used to end at a blank wall now led to the new opening into the unheated part of the house—the last stage of the entire renovation project.

Ian and his workmen cut an access into it this morning. Before he left for the weekend, he taped plastic sheeting over the gap in the wall to keep the heat in the restored main house. But as a barrier against the twins, mere plastic was worse than useless. He needn't have bothered.

"Amy! Alexander! Get back here this instant!" She hurried in the direction of the twins' voices. Since they constantly traded off the nicknames Trouble and Double-Trouble, she had no doubt they'd ignored Ian's advice and her orders to stay out of that wing until he declared it structurally sound and safe. The twins, like most kids their age, could be curious and heedless of danger.

"Aw, Mom!" Amy's voice echoed up the hallway, dripping with disdain for her parent's concern. The older by three minutes, she had her father's adventurous nature, the same drive that had them living in an old ruin in Scotland instead of on the beach in California. "We have a flashlight."

Lara laid a hand against the stone arch at the entrance to the hallway, reluctant to venture past the warm glow of the kitchen lights painting the hallway walls. "I don't care if Ian left on overhead lights in there. Get back here, right now. Ian said to stay out of there."

"There's nothing in here," Amy argued. "Come see!"

The change in her daughter's tone from disagreement to invitation was so heartening, Lara actually took a few steps down the hall. But unless the twins started screaming, she couldn't bring herself to go through the plastic barrier into the dark. No telling what might actually be lurking there. She shuddered at the idea of a ghost roaming these halls. Granted, being superstitious about this old estate seemed…silly. She wasn't afraid, exactly. She just didn't like dark places. Trying not to communicate her concern too strongly, she kept her tone light when she responded. "If there's nothing in there, then there's nothing to see. Come on, kids." When they didn't respond right away, she added more sharply, "Now!"

"We're coming." That from Alexander.

She could picture Alex, ever the peacemaker, grabbing his sister's hand. Bless him. Left to her own devices, Amy would balk, but Alex had a way with her that prevented a lot of mother-daughter battles since they'd lost Angus.

She stepped back into the kitchen and pulled a bottle of milk from the refrigerator. She was reaching for a saucepan when the twins appeared, covered in dust and, in Amy's case, defiance. Alex held the flashlight. Lara guessed he'd threatened to leave Amy behind in the dark.

Whatever worked.

"Ian told you not to go in there," she scolded. "And now look at you. You've got dirt and dust all over you, and you're tracking it on my clean floor."

They both studied the floor tiles.

"Look," she said, setting aside the saucepan and planting her hands on her hips, "I don't care about a little dirt, but I do care about both of you. I don't want something to happen to you." Maybe laying on the guilt would work where ordering them to stay out had not. "Promise me you won't go back in there until Ian says it's safe."

Alex nodded first, then Amy.

Okay, maybe they'd pay attention this time. Chances were slim, but she could hope—and keep her mommy radar set on max. Time for a little positive reinforcement. "So, now that you're straight on the rules, anybody up for hot cocoa?"

Their heads snapped up, and they glanced at each other, blinking in the kitchen's overhead light, then back to her. She could almost hear them thinking, All right! She's not that mad.

"I am!" Alex elbowed his sister in the side. "Amy is, too."

Amy nodded.

Well, good. "Go get cleaned up. Your cocoa will be ready by the time you get back."

Alex dropped the flashlight on the counter, and the twins took off at a run for their rooms.

Lara got out the cocoa, sugar, and vanilla, mixed the ingredients together with the milk in the saucepan, set it on the stove to heat and gave it an occasional stir, her mind still on what might lie beyond the flimsy plastic barrier.

The three-story manor had been unoccupied for decades until she and her late husband bought it. Angus had some romantic notion about his family hailing from this part of Scotland, though more than a century ago, they left to make their fortune in America. The moment he'd laid eyes on the ancient stone of the seventeenth century wing anchoring the north side, he'd fallen in love with the old ruin. The restoration, not to mention paying the taxes, was possible only because of her family money. Renovations on the eighteenth century main house and south wing went on for months to finish enough livable space for them to move into last summer. The eat-in kitchen and their bedrooms had been first on his list. Knowing her love of books, he'd finished the library soon after. Angus had done some of the work, but mostly he'd managed the numerous contractors needed to bring an estate like this back to habitable condition. Late last September, he started renovating the dining hall and a neighboring room she planned to use as a parlor.

Ian finished them.

This week, he turned his attention to the older north wing, explaining the previous owners had probably sealed it off from the new structures because they didn't need the space and didn't want to maintain it. Though the realtor who'd shown the property suggested they should probably knock it down, she looked forward to seeing what surprises it held. Places this old always had something unexpected within a wall or a floor. After what Ian told her, she secretly hoped Cairn Dubh would, too. Ian had spent today measuring all the ground floor rooms and seemed unsurprised when they didn't match up against the outside dimension of the structure, even accounting for the thickness of the walls. He'd explained there might be at least one hidden room—not an unusual occurrence in very old structures.

"I suspect I'll be spending more time at Cairn Dubh until I know precisely what I'm dealing with," he'd said.

Her body had greeted his news with a spike of heat and longing that still surprised her. Lately, her interest in Ian began to extend beyond the restoration. As though she was coming out of the year-long fog of grief, she started to pay attention to his voice, his mannerisms, his looks. Having those feeling stir for another man made her palms sweat.

She knew she wasn't betraying Angus, but on some level, guilt made her want to avoid Ian altogether, though she knew that was impossible. On another level, she wanted to see more of him. Lots more of him. She guessed Ian to be no more than three or four years her senior. He was taller than Angus had been and more muscular. She presumed years of working construction would account for his delicious build. His hair brushed his collar in a lovely shade of warm auburn that glowed with copper streaks when it caught the light.

Her fingers tingled with the need to touch it. Was it as soft as it looked? She found herself wanting to run them through its thick length. His features were as finely crafted as the work he did, and his amber eyes were often filled with laughter too long missing from Cairn Dubh. The laughter lifted his full lips into a grin or a smile, depending on whether he was talking to his workmen or the twins. Or her. Lips she found herself wanting to touch. And taste. But she had to keep her cool. She hated the clingy widow stereotype and refused to go there. If anything developed between her and Ian, it would have to do so in its own sweet time.

She sighed and stirred the cocoa again. Not that she'd be doing anything like that any time soon. Angus had been gone less than a year. The week before All Hallows. Damn him for saddling them with that anniversary to remember each October. At home in California, the twins loved Halloween, which, she realized with a start, was in a couple of weeks. Well, she would have to make sure the twins enjoyed it here this year—somehow. The Scots had originated trick-or-treating hundreds of years ago and still celebrated it, though with less enthusiasm—and less sugar —than in her old neighborhood. Maybe Becky could tell her what she needed to do.

She made a mental note to check with her friend, and to call home next week. Her parents would worry if they didn't hear from her on this anniversary. She knew her mother would pester her about finding a new man, and that was a discussion she dreaded. She might be attracted to Ian, and she had been alone almost a year...but he'd given no indication he might return her interest. Or had he?

She'd noticed how he smiled at her and watched her as she inspected the work his contractors had done. More than once, she'd noticed his gaze linger. At first, she'd thought he was only interested in her approval, but then he'd lean in close to point out some detail, and she'd find herself drawn to his scent and his heat. He'd never touched her, except to shake her hand, but every once in a while, she got the sense he'd like to.

Would she like him to touch her? To kiss her? Much to her surprise, she thought she would. She couldn't decide if it felt too soon, or if these heated stirrings meant she was ready to get on with her life. To meet men. To date. Even to take another man to her bed.

Maybe once Ian finished the restoration, if she still felt the same, she'd find a way to let him know she welcomed his attention. But not until then. As she took the cocoa off the stove and called the twins, she made her decision.

Ian had to be off limits for as long as he was on her payroll.

CHAPTER 2

The next day, the twins' laughter drifted in Lara MacLaren's open bedroom window, clear, bright and given what she'd decided to do today, a welcome counterpoint to her mood. Instead of the clouds that had blanketed this part of Scotland for weeks, this October Saturday was sunny and warm. Alex and Amy had rushed outside as soon as they finished breakfast. She didn't blame them. It was too nice out to stay inside. But she'd put this chore off long enough.

Lara could hear them chasing each other through crunching leaves, Amy shrieking and Alex laughing. She leaned out of the window for a moment and watched as Alex tagged Amy, then they took off again, Amy in pursuit of her brother.

Lara smiled, then turned back to her room. Her task was here. She didn't know why today of all days she'd decided to tackle going through Angus's closet, but perhaps the sunshine had something to do with it. She couldn't have faced sorting through his things on a gloomy day.

We never even had a chance to say goodbye.

The thought always made her chest feel like a hollowed-out shell, dry, brittle and ready to shatter into a thousand pieces.

She carried a packing box into his walk-in closet and took a breath. The faint scent of Angus's cologne—and Angus—lingered, nearly bringing tears to her eyes, but she fought them back. She was past tears, and she'd chosen to tackle his closet now because a sunny day was not the time for them.

She set the box aside and ran a hand over the shoulders of his suits, hung neatly and undisturbed for all these months. The newest, an appropriately subtle Harris Tweed, had been his favorite, but he'd left it behind on his last trip. In California, he would have roasted in it, though surely taking it must have crossed his mind. Wearing it, he looked every inch the proper Scottish gentleman. His fascination with his heritage had brought them here, and he would have enjoyed playing the part with the friends and business contacts he'd left behind.

A new kilt in the MacLaren tartan hung toward the back. He'd never worn it. Only for special occasions he'd said. Like a big anniversary party or wedding. She'd spent their last wedding anniversary without him.

His silk ties hung neatly on a revolving rack. She gave it a spin, then moved on to his built-in drawers. The upper ones were filled with underwear. The lower ones contained sweaters, a few heavy wool ones for the coldest winter days, but mostly cashmere. She pulled out a lower drawer and fingered a cashmere sweater's fine, soft texture, deciding to save them all for Alex, along with the kilt. Sweaters never went out of style. Annie might want one or two, as well. She closed that drawer and opened an upper one, then started filling the box with T-shirts. Someone could use those and Angus's socks, no matter the time of year.

For months, though she was grateful they were well off, she would have gladly traded every penny to have him back. Lately, the strength of her yearning for him was beginning to fade, and although she supposed that was another step in the grieving process, it unsettled her. She did not want to forget any part of him: his voice, his touch, the way he doted on the twins. His scent. She held a T-shirt up to her nose, but inhaled nothing more than the fragrance of laundry soap. No trace of Angus remained. She tossed the shirt into the box and reached for the rest of the stack.

After she filled a few boxes, she realized it had gotten quiet. She went to the window to check on the twins. Her heart leapt when she spotted them, side-by-side, unmoving, facing the woods behind the house. They didn't look frightened. Fascinated, maybe. Awestruck? What did they see?

It took Lara a moment to find the big stag in the midst of the undergrowth. The bare trees were probably the only reason she could see his body. His antlers looked like branches and twigs. Earlier in the year, he would have been completely hidden by leaves. For a moment, she thought the twins and the stag were in a staredown. Thank goodness the big buck wasn't advancing on them. She couldn't imagine it would hurt them, but since it was rutting season and it used those antlers to fight other stags, anything was possible.

The twins turned to each other and whispered something.

Lara frowned, surprised, when the stag didn't react to their movement. Then she realized its gaze fastened not on the twins, but on the old north wing of the house. Suddenly, it turned and bolted into the woods. She heard it crashing through the undergrowth in its haste to get away.

The twins calling "Wow!" and "Mom, did you see that?" pulled her attention back to them. "I did," she answered and waved. "Wasn't he magnificent!"

"He sure was big," Alex remarked, then took off toward the woods.

"Alex, get back here!" Lara called, concerned. "Do not chase that stag into the woods." When she saw Alex circle back toward the house, she relaxed. "You couldn't catch him, anyway," she muttered under her breath.

Alex rejoined his sister. "I wanted to see where he went."

Annie shoved her brother. "That's dumb. He didn't care about us," she taunted, then turned her face up to her mother. "How cool is that?"

"No, he sure didn't," Lara said, mulling over how the stag had appeared and where his attention had seemed to be—on the north wing. What did the stag see or sense in that old structure?

~

Saturday evening, Ian Paterson straightened up from where he'd been leaning against the bar in MacGinty's pub, swallowed his surprise, and hoisted his whisky to toast his friend. "Sláinte, Blane. May she say yes, and may ye have many happy years together."

Blane gestured at the open ring box on the bar with the bottle of single malt whisky in his hand. Before sharing his news and showing off the rock he planned to give his girlfriend, Cassie, he'd poured drinks for the lads he'd invited to the pub this evening.

"She'd better. I can't face the idea of taking it back to the jeweler. He'll laugh his arse off."

Ian looked at the friends surrounding them and grinned. "Well, he'll not be laughing alone."

Blane tossed back the dregs in his glass and choked as he tried to join in the chuckles following Ian's comment. After a moment, he cleared his throat. "What about ye? I hear the widow you're working for is beyond bonnie."

Ian stiffened, then reminded himself this was Blane's party, and he didn't mean anything by his comment. Still, Ian found he couldn't let it go. "She's my employer at the moment, and ye ken how important this restoration is to me." He lifted his glass. "I'll thank ye to have some respect." He grinned to soften the rebuke.

"Does she ken?"

"What? Nay. And ye lot," Ian said, giving the rest of the men drinking with them an uncharacteristically forbidding frown, "will not be telling her a thing."

"But…"

"Not a word. She has enough to worry her."

"And she has twins," Thomas interjected.

"Instant family," Colin added with a shudder.

"Quit yer haiverin'. The twins are fine," Ian informed him, then remembered his intent to keep things light and rolled his eyes. "If I can keep them out of the construction areas, they might survive to reach puberty. I make no guarantees after that."

The men laughed and went back to drinking Blane's whisky. Soon, their conversations amped up the noise level, and Blane leaned closer.

"O' course, we haven't set a date," Blane said and lifted his glass. "But when the time comes, milord, I'd be honored if ye'd be my best man."

"I'd be honored to stand with you," Ian answered and clinked his glass against Blane's, then took the expected sip. "If you can get through the whole thing without calling me that."

"Aye, well, and Cassie will be thrilled to have ye as part of our wedding."

"You won't let her make too much of it—"

"Nay, of course not. Anyway, she'll be dying to ken who you'll bring."

Ian leaned against the bar, his thoughts full of twin redheaded hellions and their all-too-attractive mother. He'd been spending more time at Cairn Dubh than strictly necessary, not that he'd admit it to these lads. He should have no trouble focusing on his work on the keep, but Lara MacLaren distracted him. Blonde and willowy, with a musical laugh and a firm, but fair, way with her children, she intruded into his thoughts constantly. He had never let a client become more to him than a paycheck, but he couldn't stop watching her, or thinking about her. Though he knew he needed to keep his distance, staying away from her and keeping his focus on her house where it belonged was becoming more difficult every day. Yet he dared not let on he'd like to get to know her better, not if he wanted to keep this job. And he did.

He grimaced and forced his attention back to Blane. He gestured at the ring box, now closed, still sitting on the bar. "When are ye going to ask her?"

"Tomorrow, after kirk. We're going to her parents' for Sunday dinner."

"You're certain they'll approve?"

"Aye. I've already spoken to her da. It's all arranged."

Ian lifted his glass and tipped it toward Blane in salute. "Good man."

"Good enough, I hope." Blane pocketed the box and added, "She's…special."

Ian shook his head. "You only met her six months ago. How do you know she's the one?" His question came from simple curiosity, nothing more. Certainly nothing to do with his bonnie employer.

Blane shrugged. "I can't say. It's not like I knew the first moment I saw her. It took a month or two."

"A month or two…" Ian repeated, shaking his head. "For a lifetime commitment."

"A month or two," Blane agreed with a wave of his

hand. "Then I knew. Just like you will when the time…and the lass…is right."

The vision of a tall lass with red-haired twins appeared before Ian's eyes. He blinked away the image and finished his whisky with a gulp that burned all the way down. If only it would burn away his fascination with Lara MacLaren.

CHAPTER 3

*L*ara was sure schoolday Monday mornings were the same everywhere. The twins always fussed and fought her every step of the way, from the time she rousted them out of bed before sunrise until she delivered them to school. Today, they settled down some over breakfast, muttering to each other in their unintelligible twin-speak, with only the occasional pronoun—he, in this case—coming through in the clear. Who were they talking about? The stag? Scamp the cat? Ian? She noticed Amy's gaze kept straying to the hallway leading to the newly opened wing.

She had no doubt they were plenty interested in the rooms over there. Kids loved to explore. She had, too, at the same age, so it could simply be the draw of a new territory. Still, they'd been warned to keep out until Ian gave the okay. So why all the unintelligible chatter? Were they planning to sneak over there when no one else was around?

She'd have to get Ian to give her a tour when she returned from dropping off the twins. Not only would she satisfy her curiosity about the rooms in that wing— and the potential dangers to the twins—she'd get to spend some time alone with him. Maybe she would be able to get him to talk about himself a little. He hadn't revealed anything significant about his personal life in the time he'd been working on Cairn Dubh. Though she shouldn't, she wanted…even needed…to know more.

As she was herding the twins out of the house to the car, Ian and another man arrived, which added another delay while he crouched down to greet the children. He impressed Lara with how he tolerated, with exceedingly good grace, being tugged on and jabbered at in stereo. The twins' determination to delay their departure didn't seem to faze him. After a few moments, he stood, Alex in one arm, Amy in the other, their feet dangling at half their height above ground.

"Behave yerselves," he told first one, then the other, laying on a thicker-than-usual Scots accent and rolling his r's. He directed a wink Lara's way before adding, "And learn everything ye can from your teachers, or I'll turn ye upside down next time." To a chorus of shrieks and laughter, he set them on their feet and gently shoved them toward their mother.

Lara gave him a grateful smile. She also nodded to his older companion as she ushered her troublemakers away. Before she started the engine, she noticed Ian's gaze on the car, a wistful expression on his face. What was going through his mind? She was fairly certain he was unmarried and, as far as she knew, childless. Among the many things he'd never mentioned, he never mentioned a wife or a family. And so far, she hadn't found a plausible reason to ask. The last thing she wanted was for him to think she was prying into his personal life. But still, she wished she knew—was he thinking about her or about the twins? Or just admiring the car?

His companion clapped him on the back and said something that made him turn away. She wrenched her gaze from him and drove off. She had to get her wild imaginings under control. She needed to focus on her job, which didn't include ogling Ian's remarkable ass, at least not until she finished driving her children safely to school. Even then, she had no business thinking about Ian in that way. Not until he finished the restoration. Off limits, she reminded herself. Damn it.

"Are we there yet?" Alex crowed after they'd gone a mile. She laughed because he expected her to, even though thoughts of Ian's muscled arms and tightly rounded backside still distracted her.

"Sooner than you'll like, me laddie-bucko," she answered in a pirate's drawl, giving Alex the usual response for a schoolday trip.

At the school, she pulled into the parking lot, or car park, as it was called here. The twins were still young enough not to object too much to her goodbye kiss. Then they ran for the front door of the school, intent on getting out of the snow just beginning to drift down, and fell in with the other kids headed the same way.

She got back in the car and stared at the swirling flakes, seeing only Ian.

What did she know about him, really? Damn little was ever said about his background or family by anyone. In town, she only got nods and smiles if she mentioned he was in charge of the restoration at Cairn Dubh. The Scots could be quite close-mouthed when they wanted to.

Ian was reliable. He never missed a workday, check. First to arrive, last to leave, check. Great with the twins, oh yes, check. That one gave her a twinge, deep inside where her heart used to be, before Angus took it to the grave with him. Any man who wanted her would have to love her twins, and they him. Ian already seemed to like them, thank God. If they thought he disliked them, they would make no end of trouble—as only her twins could do. She knew the twins were fascinated with him. Or was it just because he controlled their access to the mysterious parts of the estate? Time would tell. At any rate, she loved seeing him interact with them. Polite to her, check. More than polite? She had to be imagining anything else.

But maybe not. She could dream…and hope for more. When the time was right. With a shrug, she put the car in gear and drove home.

~

When Ian heard Lara call his name, his breath caught. He hadn't heard her car come up the drive to the keep, but he'd been focused on what Rollo Hay, his structural engineer, had found in what appeared to be a closet or privy at the far side of the old wing's ground floor. The slate flooring tiles were loose and a few lay at slight angles, out of place. Could someone have filled in a well or trash pit and laid the tiles over it? Unusual to find such a thing inside a seventeenth century dwelling, to say the least. Rollo would investigate it eventually, but his first order of business was to make sure there were no problems with the building's foundation.

He left Rollo and went to meet Lara. She'd paused where they broke through the wall. Good. He didn't want her alone in here anymore than he wanted the twins running loose until he'd found and eliminated any dangers. So far, they'd only strung lights on this level. He hadn't had a chance to check the upper floors yet, but oddly, what he'd seen on the ground floor didn't live up to its "the old wing's about to fall into ruin" reputation. Rollo had declared the joists over their heads had held up well enough. He and Ian could work safely in the space. Rollo was damn good at his job, but Ian would check everything himself before he put Lara and the twins at risk.

She'd been gone less than an hour—barely long enough to drive the twins to school and back. Since he'd taken over the restoration, she'd rarely intruded during the work day, so for her to show up now, she must be as curious as her children about this wing. "It's okay," he told her. "You can come ahead."

She nodded and took a few cautious steps into the room, scuffing her shoes on the stone floor and turning her head to take in the space, making her bright hair skim the tops of her shoulders.

Ian's fingers itched to brush back the last few strands and run his fingertips from her shoulders up along her neck, then grasp the back of her head and pull her into a kiss. Thank God, she wasn't looking in his direction, or she might see the hunger for her in his eyes.

"I wonder what the builders used this area for."

Pulling his attention away from the golden glints in her hair and giving her a nonchalant shrug took every ounce of willpower he possessed. "Storage, most likely. Living and sleeping chambers above." Lara's nearness made Ian think sleeping chambers meant beds…and beds were not just for sleeping, even all those centuries ago.

Her gaze swept the room and the ceiling, as if she tried to picture how the spaces Ian named would be laid out, then settled back on him. The room suddenly heated. Lara shifted her stance, then glanced away.

Ian stared, wondering how to break the tension growing between them. "Why don't I show you around?" he offered. That would keep her with him. He could enjoy looking at her, hearing her voice, and feeling her near him, if only for a few more minutes. Rollo was sure to interrupt all too soon.

"If it's okay," she answered, a spark of curiosity bright in her eyes as her head came around and she met his gaze. Then she glanced around again and sighed. "Angus would have loved this. It's a shame he never got to see it."

Christ, that took some of the heat out of the room. Ian's jaw clenched. He resented the mention of her late husband, especially after the way he'd been thinking about her just moments ago. And because not getting this job a year ago stung. Angus had never told him why, though Ian was pretty sure he knew the reason. Someone had mentioned Ian's connection to the place.

Lara's call to come take over the restoration had surprised him. Chances were, Angus never told her about him, and for that, Ian was very glad.

"Follow me," he told her, his tone more gruff than he intended. Still, the reminder of her late husband chafed. He forced Angus out of his mind and led Lara down the ground floor's main hallway.

He pointed out the structural features as he led her through the secondary rooms on this level, including the one with the odd area of flooring. Rollo stood and dusted off his hands when Ian introduced him. Lara offered her hand.

He grasped her fingers briefly. "Missus."

"It's lovely to meet you, Mr. Hay. By the way," Lara asked, "have you seen any sign of a mouse down here?"

"Nay, lassie." He patted the wall at his side. "The wee beastie'd have a hard time coming in through this much stone."

Her smile seemed a bit…confused. Did she think mice could gnaw through the mortar?

Rollo went back to examining the base of the wall as Ian led her away.

As they approached the main stairway, Lara asked, "Can we go upstairs? I'm curious to see how people lived before the newer part of the house was built."

Ian nodded, happy to spend more time with her, then paused, considering. "There's nothing wrong with the stone steps, and Rollo thinks the floor joists are sound, but we haven't been up there yet. I don't know what we'll find."

"Then let's explore together," she said with a hint of a smile. "Unless I'm keeping you from something you need to be doing." She held up a hand. "I'm sorry. I don't mean to take up all of your time this morning."

"You're not intruding. I'm happy to show you around."

Her answering smile lit up the dark spaces in Ian's heart. The pain of that illumination surprised him. He'd thought he'd moved past his own grief over the loss last year of the grandfather who'd raised him after his parents died in an auto accident when he was nine. He supposed that was one reason he got along with Lara's twins—he knew firsthand what they were going through. But his grandfather had not lived to wander these halls as Ian was about to. Life wasn't fair. His grandfather had been certain their heritage lay within these walls. If it existed, Ian might be on the verge of finding it, but he'd never be able to share it with the one person to whom it would have meant the most.

He shook his head and pulled his attention back to the woman at his side.

Lara looked around them, her face alive with curiosity.

Ian couldn't help returning her smile, even though his experience told him even the most benign-looking structures could harbor a nasty surprise or two. "Only if you will stay by me and not wander off." He grabbed two torches from a nearby work table and stuck one in his back pocket. "We haven't strung lights up there yet."

Lara suddenly looked uncertain. "Of course. You're in charge."

Ian would have paid good coin to know what went through her mind just then. Instead of asking, he switched on his torch, and started up the worn stone steps. "Have a care. They're not even close to being level any longer."

"I see that. Think of all the footfalls it took to make these dips in the stone."

"Thousands. Thousands of thousands, probably."

"This is the oldest part of the keep, isn't it?" Lara asked after they reached the next level.

"That we've found." Ian played the beam of light around them. The floors looked sound, the boards level and unwarped. He didn't see any water stains on the walls or on the joists high above their heads. "Probably the original structure, which explains the lack of windows on the lower level, for defense. It's odd that someone took the trouble to brick up every opening, including sealing the whole thing off from the newer construction. Even odder that over the centuries, no one opened it up again."

"Maybe the newer part was more comfortable to live in, so they just left the drafty old wing alone."

"Maybe." Ian swept the torch's beam toward the ceiling. "This area was probably the original great hall. It's too large to have been anything else. The height of the ceiling means the upper floor has a smaller footprint, and wraps around this space."

Lara took a few steps toward the nearest doorway, surveying what Ian's torch revealed. "It is strange that no one has tried to get in here lately—whether lately means decades or centuries."

"This has always been private property, well off the main road and not easy to get to."

She crossed her arms and shivered as she peered into the empty space over her head. "It's more than a little spooky up here now."

Was she cold? Or afraid of the dark? He'd give her the other torch, but he wanted her to stay right with him. If she had her own light, she might wander away and get into trouble. "It'll be better once we clear the bricks from the windows and let in some sunshine and air."

"How long will that take?"

"Not long, once Rollo approves the structure around them. But we'll need to cover them with plastic, or glass them in quickly. The wet will ruin the floors in a hurry." He glanced upward, though there was nothing to see but the underside of the floor above them. "'Tis a miracle the roof is still on. Roofed structures were once so heavily taxed, owners removed them from buildings no one lived in."

"Is that why so many castles are in ruins?"

"It's one reason," he replied, resisting the temptation to mention how many had been destroyed in battles or pulled down to prevent English forces from occupying Scottish territory. "Whoever built the main house actually re-roofed this old wing to match the rest."

"And yet didn't bother to open up this wing. That is strange."

Ian took Lara's arm and led her to one of the doorways off the great hall's open space, enjoying her nearness and how the light, fresh scent she wore distracted him from the dust and must of the age-old stone and wood surrounding them. He played the torch around the room, but it was empty. Lara shrugged, and they moved to the next. It, too, was empty. The floors continued to be sound, so he suggested, "Let's go up," and lit her way back to the stone stairs.

Lara glanced up the stairway and shrugged. "Let's," she said and started up the steps ahead of him.

Though he kept the light on the uneven stones at her feet, she suddenly stumbled and softly cried out. Ian grabbed for her and got an arm around her waist before her knees banged into the step above. She sucked in a breath when he pulled her back against his body and held her there. He meant only to give her a moment to get her feet back under her but found he could not let her go. Instead, he wrapped both arms around her, annoyed he could only touch her with one hand. The other held their light source.

"Are ye okay?" Ian felt Lara's ribs expand under his hand as she breathed.

"I am now," she murmured. "I could have sprained an ankle, or fallen and hit my head."

"You needn't worry," he answered softly. "I've got you." Pressed against his hard length, right where he needed her. Though he knew holding her was a mistake, he couldn't let her go.

Her face flushed. "You do at that. I...I..." She glanced at the ceiling, then returned her gaze to his. "Thank you..."

"You're welcome. I don't mind a bit," Ian teased. Her

body was firm, yet soft against his. She made no move to escape his embrace. He lowered his gaze to her mouth. Her lips were so close. So tempting.

Lara's breath warmed his face. Her gaze met his, then dropped quickly to his mouth.

He was certain she meant to allow his kiss…and to kiss him back. He parted his lips, drinking in her scent, eager to taste her.

Something moved in the darkness below them, soundless, but stirring the cool air and whispering across his hands. The back of Ian's neck prickled.

Lara stiffened and cocked her head, as if listening. "Just a draft," he murmured. Ian could have sworn it was only moving air, nothing more. He hoped. He'd grown up hearing tales about Cairn Dubh—and its ghost. If Cairn Dubh did have a ghost, this ancient space would be a fine place for it to haunt.

He felt certain Lara would not enjoy hearing that. "Maybe Rollo went outside," he offered, hoping to ease her tension and perhaps even get back to the kiss that seemed inevitable only moments ago.

Her expression grew serious and she pulled away. "That did not feel like the breeze from an open door. I want to go see what caused it."

Reluctantly, he let her go. "Very well. Then you can go on about your day, if you like. We'll save the upper floors for another time."

CHAPTER 4

On the way into town the next day, the twins stayed quiet on the ride to school. Perfect timing, as far as Lara was concerned. After tossing and turning all night, she still wanted to kick herself. She had no business getting so close to Ian. She'd practically thrown herself at him, turning in his arms at his slightest touch. Suddenly hungry to feel hard male muscles against her curves, she'd pressed against him. She couldn't miss the thudding of his heartbeat thundering in his chest. Her heart beat even faster, spurred on by his heat and the solid strength of his arms around her as he pulled her tightly against him. She'd discovered his hair was as soft and thick as she'd imagined, and she'd reveled in the feel of him hardening against her thigh when he realized she was touching him, even if she was merely caressing his hair. His gaze had bored into her as though he tried to read her thoughts, her intentions. And those lips. She'd been tempted to taste them. Too tempted.

Thank goodness Rollo had gone outside when he did. That breath of air from a door opening had distracted them from…what? She couldn't bear thinking about how close they'd come to that kiss. She could deny the rest of what she'd felt—and what he'd felt—but a kiss would have been unmistakable. Undeniable. And it would have changed everything.

However, thanks to Rollo's trip out to his truck, which was the only thing she could think of to explain the weird draft she'd felt, she'd pulled back at the last second, before she made a complete and utter fool of herself.

What had happened to her decision to make Ian off limits?

She'd let her body's burgeoning demands confuse her. And she'd confused him. She could see it—and maybe even anger—in his eyes. But ever the gentleman, he'd let her go and led her down the stairs, ready to save her if she lost her footing again.

If only he could save her from herself.

She was an idiot. She really didn't want to do anything to make him think of her as a desperate, lonely widow. She couldn't. She needed him to finish this restoration. If she scared him off, Cairn Dubh would never be finished. No one else had been interested in a project of this magnitude. She'd never be able to sell it and return to California.

Lara sucked in a breath. Sell this place and return to California? Where had that thought come from? A vision of miles of taillights in stalled traffic suddenly overlaid her view of pine trees and the empty two-lane road. She hadn't been tempted by the thought of returning home in months, not since soon after Angus's death. Why now?

She'd never really thought about what came next, she realized. She'd been in a daze since Angus died. When she decided she had to finish the project they'd started, she'd never considered what she'd do once it was done. The twins loved living here. As much as they complained about school, they liked their teachers and the other kids. She didn't have to worry about money. So what had made leaving pop into her head?

Was it because she was attracted to Ian Paterson? Ridiculous! Sure, he was tall, good-looking, and the only man she'd spent significant time with in the last year, but seriously, she needed to stop imagining that she was attracted to him, or him to her. Their embrace didn't mean anything except that he'd saved her from a fall. Her fog of grief was lifting, and that was all. If she wasn't careful, every man in town would start to look good to her.

Yet she knew she was kidding herself. The only man who looked good to her was Ian Paterson, the one man whose masculine pull she had to ignore. She pictured him wearing heavy glasses held together with white tape; a battered notebook, and not the digital kind, in his hand; and a collection of pencils and pens sticking out of a shirt pocket. When that image failed to do more than make her want to laugh, Lara sighed and put Ian firmly out of her mind. She reached the village, dropped the twins at school, and headed for the co-op market, running her shopping list through her mind like a litany.

Her friend Becky waved as she got out of her car. "I'm

glad to see you," she said. "I was going to call you later to remind you about the big harvest market day this weekend. Craftsmen from all around the area will be there, as well as the farmers. Have you been to a market day before?"

Lara shook her head. "No, not yet." She took it as a sign of her improving outlook that a day in the festival atmosphere of market day finally sounded like fun. And it would be good for the twins, she reasoned.

"Well, you must not miss this one," Becky told her. "The farmers will have turnips for making jack-o'-lanterns," she said.

"I'm glad you said that. I was going to ask you about Halloween customs."

Becky nodded, then grimaced, saying, "The Christmas and Hogmanay crafts will start to appear this month, too." She tsked and shook her head. "They show up earlier every year."

Lara laughed at the shared nonsense of holiday marketing—much the same, it seemed, on both sides of the Atlantic—and felt another layer of fog lift. "You have no idea. Winter clothes hit the stores in July in the States. Christmas decorations go up the moment Halloween is over. Sometimes before. New Year's— Hogmanay—gets a few, too, but not like Christmas."

Becky laughed with her. "At any rate, you'd enjoy it, and those two scamps of yours would, too."

Lara nodded. "I'll think about it. I'm headed for the co-op now. I need milk and bread and…well, you wouldn't believe how much two nine-year-olds can eat."

"Mine are grown, but I remember. Ach! The food those

lads could put away." As they headed up the street toward the market, Becky asked, "And how is the restoration going now Ba…I mean Ian, has taken it in hand?"

Lara's hackles rose. What nickname did Ian have that no one wanted to mention around her, but kept slipping out anyway?

"You're not the first person who's almost called Ian by another name. So fess up. What is it? A pet nickname? A team name? Something perverse that guys call each other —something he got stuck with in high school?"

Becky cleared her throat and shifted her gaze to the side. "Ach, 'tis nothing. And if you were to slip and call him by it, he'd be embarrassed, so 'tis best I not tell you."

"Oh, come on. How bad can it be?" Lara urged. She paused and planted her hands on her hips, waiting.

Becky shook her head and kept walking.

Really? Lara took two long strides and caught up with her. "Okay, you're going to make me guess," she warned. "But if I get it right, you have to tell me." She stared off into space as if contemplating the secrets of the universe. "Let's see…something embarrassing. Is he a youngest child? Baby! That must be it."

Becky pursed her lips and glanced aside at her. "Seriously? You have met the man, haven't you?"

Lara let an evil laugh bubble up, and Becky joined in. Then she got back to business. "So, not baby. How about sports…hmmm, ball hog?"

No reaction.

"Bad ass, that's it, right? You said embarrassing." Becky's lips twitched but she shook her head.

"He's got a fine one, but no, that's not it either."

Lara snickered right along with her, the image of Ian's backside filling her mind for the moment. Don't go there! She needed to stop thinking about Ian that way. And Becky had an uncanny ability to read her like a book. Lara wouldn't have to drool to reveal how her interest in Ian had grown—and changed. Stick to business—this was a close as she'd come to finding out one of Ian's secrets. "No? Wait, what's that Scottish word I've heard a few times? Ah, I've got it! Bampot."

Becky giggled but kept shaking her head.

"Really? Good. I can't see anyone calling him an idiot. What else…certainly not bastard."

Becky choked and stopped walking. Her hand flew up to cover her mouth, her shoulders shaking with mirth. "Nay."

"Well, thank goodness."

Becky held up her hand and Lara paused to let her catch her breath from laughing.

"No, and nay. You're way off."

They started walking again, but Lara had run dry of words that sounded like they started with "b-a." She'd try out others as she thought of them. Becky wasn't going to get off so easily. "Tell me more about the market day," she requested, conceding defeat for the moment and changing the subject as they arrived at the door of the co-op market.

Becky dipped her head, indicating the interior of the store. "Don't buy any more here than you'll need between now and then. The harvest is coming in. The farmers will bring fresh-picked produce right from the field. Stock up with them."

"Okay, that sounds like good advice."

"Brilliant. Now, I'm off to find where I left my car. I've run so many errands today, I've lost track, and I've got to get home and get some cleaning done." With a wave, she added, "I'll see you this weekend. Cheers."

"I hope so," Lara replied. No, she would. Anniversary or not, it was time, and the twins deserved a day of fun.

After no more than another nod, Becky walked away.

Lara watched her go for a moment, suddenly wondering if she'd ever fit in here. She missed the hug she would have gotten from one of her friends in California when they parted. She missed her friends, her parents, sunshine—oh, she had to stop this. She'd made the decision to stay, at least through the restoration and possible sale of the house, and maybe forever. If she went back to California, she'd miss Scotland, the people here, and especially, she feared, Ian Paterson. That was life. Gaining and losing, often when you least expected it. Either way, she'd adjust. They all would. For now, she'd better focus on why she came to town. An hour later, grocery shopping done, she stopped at the petrol station to put gas in the car and then headed home.

~

Ian's mobile rang, breaking his concentration on the plan he was drawing up to restore the great hall on the first floor of Cairn Dubh's oldest wing. Since the place wasn't exactly, as rumored, one strong wind away from falling down, he'd turned to thinking about its interior. And no matter how he measured, using his father's metal measuring tape or his new laser tool, the interior dimensions were off. There had to be a hidden space—or more than one—in the void he'd left on his plan, a void that was repeated on each floor of the old wing.

While he shifted his seat on the stool and pulled his mobile from his back pocket, he reminded himself to make sure Lara knew to keep the twins out until Rollo finished the foundation work. He'd mulled over the idea of closing the wing off from the house again and cutting a construction opening on an outside wall. But the original builders would have been horrified at leaving it vulnerable to invaders. He nearly chuckled at the thought. Invaders. Right. Mice, maybe.

"Ian Paterson..." he answered.

"Good day, milord."

Blane's usual greeting made Ian groan. "Are you never going to tire of that?"

"Of course not, milord."

Ian groaned again, as expected, then huffed out a breath. "Okay, what do you need?"

"Still the most astute man I know," Blane answered, then paused.

Something was up. If Blane had a simple request, he'd be halfway through making it by now. Ian decided to wait him out.

"Okay, here's the thing. We've decided to elope."

"Shite, really? Elope?" Ian laid aside his pen and leaned

his elbows on the slanted surface of the drafting table. "That is a surprise. What's your hurry? The lass doesn't look to be about to have your love child." Ian heard a choking sound through the phone.

"You ken Cassie's family is all for this marriage…"

"So you said."

"But they want to make a huge production out of it. White gown, flowers, rent the nearest castle, the whole bit."

"And Cassie doesn't?"

"You guessed it. They've got her *scunnered*. So we're going to nip all of their nonsense in the bud and do the blacksmith thing tomorrow. Before lunch. Problem is…"

"It's a workday, and you need witnesses."

"It is, and we do. I ken it's short notice—"

"I'll be there. But are you sure you won't be burning your bridge with her family? They won't like this."

"Thanks. You're a mate. We'll find out once the deed is done. This was Cassie's idea. She knows her family. She says they'll get past it in a year or two— which will give us a year or two without demands for a grandchild."

Ian had to chuckle at that "Well, then, it appears the lass kens what she's doing."

Blane laughed, too. "Aye. Another thing—do you think that lass you're working for would be willing to come, as well? Everyone we know who wouldn't spill the plan to Cassie's family will be at their jobs, but we need at least two witnesses."

Ian drummed on his drafting table with a pencil while he thought. Was this an opportunity, or a disaster in the making? A lass might expect certain things of a man who took her to a wedding, things he knew were not wise. The job was most important. Until it was done, until he had a chance to discover whether the keep held any answers… nay, he couldn't risk it. But he wanted to. And this was Blane asking. Ian was only the messenger, aye? This might be his best chance to spend time with Lara away from the job. To get to know her better. To see if she might be interested in him—for later. After he had his answers. He took a breath, then said, "Her kids are in school during the day, so aye, she might." It might be the daftest thing he'd done in a long time, but… "I'll ask her, and her name is Lara MacLaren. By the way, why not wait for the weekend?"

"Ach, nay. If Cassie's mom gets wind of this, she'll talk Cassie out of it. Best we get it done and deal with the family after."

"You're a brave man…or a damn fool. I'm not sure which, but I'll stand with you."

"You're a friend, Baron. It's an honor. You'll let me know if ye can bring the lass. We'll have a nice lunch after to celebrate and be done in time for her to pick up her kids from school."

Ian thumbed the screen to end the call and slouched into the stool's low back, turning the mobile over and over in one hand without looking at it. What did he just agree to? He knew the risk, letting his attraction to Lara MacLaren cloud his judgment. Blane was asking, he reminded himself, not him. He tossed the mobile onto the table. Shite, that was a total rationalization.

But it worked.

So, should he call Lara, or go back out to Cairn Dubh? Her image flashed before his eyes, making the decision a simple one. After nearly kissing her, some things were best done in person. He stood and pocketed the device. He'd enjoy seeing her reaction when he invited her to a wedding.

~

Ian's arrival at her door, as Lara finished putting away the groceries she'd picked up in town, surprised her. When she returned home, his truck had been missing. She figured he wanted to avoid her after what had happened on the stairs. She'd felt his desire for her, um…growing. And they'd nearly kissed, for God's sake.

Thinking about it still made her cringe—and at the same time eager to feel his arms around her again. He had to be as confused as she by her conflicting impulses. Yet here he was—though he did look a trifle uncomfortable, standing on the front portico rather than just coming in through the kitchen as he usually did. What was going on? "What are you doing out here? Come in," she invited. "I was just about to make some tea. I thought you'd gone back to your office in town."

"I had, but something important came up. I need to ask you about it, and I thought it would go better in person."

Lara frowned. "That sounds ominous." She led him toward the kitchen.

"'Tis not." He gave her a quick grin. "I have had a

request from a friend," he told her after she gestured for him to sit at the kitchen table and set about making tea.

Relief flooded her...and with it, something else... something heated. Sitting in her kitchen, Ian looked so perfectly at home, he made her ache. Made her want what she thought she'd never have again. Or not for years, anyway. But there he was, more gorgeous than any man should be and looking at her with an expression either amused or nervous—she couldn't decide which—but which pinned her in place, breathless at the longing that overtook her. She forced herself to look away for a moment, then asked, "Your friend or mine?"

"Soon both, I hope," he told her and straightened in his chair.

The electric kettle chirped, a cloud of steam escaping its spout. She poured some of the boiling water into the teapot to warm it, all the while trying to keep straight in her mind the steps to make a proper tea. Ian distracted her. She'd forgotten what it was like to feeling fluttery and lightheaded around a man. Once, Angus had the power to steal her concentration like this. But that level of intensity between them had faded long ago. It made her uncomfortable, yet hopeful, too, that she was again capable of strong feelings other than grief and pain.

She forced herself through the steps: empty the warmed teapot. Spoon in the afternoon blend she'd found in the co-op. Add boiling water and set it aside to steep.

Ian hadn't spoken, so she knew he watched her. Tingles zinged from her fingertips to her core. Did he like what he saw? She made the mistake of glancing at him over her shoulder. He'd settled back in the chair and stretched his long legs out in front of him. He looked deliciously… sprawled. It was such a masculine pose, confident and relaxed, she could barely tear her gaze away. He'd looked away as she turned. So he didn't want her to know he was checking her out? Fine. She'd just take a second to check him out. Yet staring at him wasn't helping her focus on her task. She turned back to the counter. Could she fit the top and tea cozy on the pot without dropping either of them? Something she did automatically and easily on her own suddenly seemed like an insurmountable challenge with him in the room. But she managed it with only a slight clink as the lid slid home, then faced Ian and smiled brightly.

"So what is the request?"

Ian cleared his throat and sat up.

Lara realized he was nervous. His pose had been just that…a pose. What in the world?

"I ken this is sudden," he said, then hesitated a moment before adding, "but would you like to go with me tomorrow morning to…a wedding?"

Lara dropped into the chair opposite him and did her best to keep her mouth from falling open. "A what?"

The corner of Ian's mouth quirked up. "My friend Blane and his new fiancée, Cassie, have suddenly decided to elope." He filled her in on what Blane told him on the phone. "I promised to stand with him. He asked if you'd be willing to come and be a witness, too."

"I…"

"If ye dinna wish to, I'll try to find someone else, but

most of their friends will be at their jobs. Blane asked for ye because ye dinna ken…they fear if the family finds out, they'll try to stop them."

Funny how much Ian's accent thickened when his nerves got the best of him. Lara was tempted to leave him dangling just to hear him talk.

"He offered a nice lunch after, to be done in time for ye to collect the twins from school," Ian added with a "what do you say?" lift to his shoulder, his eyebrows raised, and head tilted.

Since weddings-as-dates could be fraught with all sorts of *Are we in a relationship or not?* issues, her instincts were screaming, *You're out of your mind to even consider doing this.* But Blane had asked for her, not Ian. This wasn't going to be a date. Just a favor for a friend. She knew it shouldn't, but somehow, the distinction disappointed her. After the way Ian held her on the stairs and seemed about to kiss her, she thought if he ever finally asked her out, it would mean more to him than a favor for a friend.

Still, it was a chance to spend time with Ian and perhaps learn more about him. "How can I say no to such an offer?" she replied, then smiled to soften her response. She didn't really intend to sound flippant. Or maybe just a little. She told herself they had to start somewhere if they were going to get to know each other outside of the confines of this estate. An elopement would have to do. "I'd love to."

She jumped up and went to pour the tea, suddenly nervous. She grabbed two mugs, thinking handling delicate teacups would not suit either one of them at the moment, though drinking tea from a mug was not done in Scotland. It was a very American habit she'd yet to break.

She paused to let the idea of going to a wedding with Ian soak in. Could she handle this? The weight of the mugs in her hand brought her focus back to making tea. Milk first, she recalled, moving to the refrigerator and silently talking herself through the process to keep her mind off the man behind her. Maybe not the sort of wedding she was used to. More a justice of the peace kind of thing, over quickly. She retrieved the small pitcher of milk she kept for tea and brought it back to the counter. No, nothing implied by Ian's offer—or his friend Blane's. Even though weddings sometimes put ideas of one sort or another in men's minds. Wedding hookups were common in California. So were marriage proposals, not that she expected anything of the sort. But she couldn't help wondering if she would have reason to thank Blane later for ending her long romantic…oh, hell, call it what it was… sexual dry spell.

Suddenly, Ian was behind her, so close she could feel his heat on her back through her shirt. He reached around her and placed his hand over hers just as her fingers found the top of the sugar bowl. "Milk, no sugar," he told her, then added, "Please. Can I help you?"

Lara stilled. He only needed to wrap his arm across her breasts to cup her opposite shoulder and he could turn her into his kiss. She'd been ready on the stairs.

Hell, she was ready now. She wished he would get on with it. She glanced aside at his mouth, then up at his eyes. He met her gaze, then dropped his to her lips before he pulled away and stepped back. Lara sighed softly and turned back to the counter. With a trembling hand, she lifted the tea cozy off the pot. "Pour yours, if you would, while I fix mine."

Ian complied and took his mug back to the table without another word.

Lara stirred her tea, took a breath and leaned back against the counter, facing Ian. He sipped from his mug with a steadier hand than she possessed at the moment.

"What does one wear to an elopement?" she asked, trying for a light tone and hoping a typical female concern would set both of them more at ease.

Ian set down his mug and stared off into space as if giving her question serious consideration. "Something simple, I'd guess. I can't say for sure. I've never attended one."

The vein pulsing at his temple told her he'd been as affected by her nearness as she had by his. But if he wanted to play this cool, she could do cool. "Nor have I." She shrugged, as if nothing had passed between them. "We'll have to improvise."

She moved to the table and sat. For a few moments, silence reigned as they sipped tea and looked everywhere but at each other. Her idea of improvising with the man across the table had little to do with clothing. The less of it, the better, in fact. She pressed a hand to her mouth to block the thoughts running through her head. The symbolic censorship worked for a moment, then a clock chimed from the library and she jumped up again. "I forgot what time it is. Are you hungry? I can make a sandwich."

Ian's gaze leapt to hers from wherever his thoughts had taken him. He shook his head. "Thanks, but no. I should check on Rollo while I'm here and then get back to my office. I'm working on a plan for the original great hall as a place to start the interior work."

"That sounds…expensive."

"Not that bad. A lot will depend on how you want to finish it. Oh, and in case I didn't say this before now, I really don't want the twins in there until Rollo and I have seen to the upper floors."

His concern for her children warmed her in a place that had felt empty and cold since Angus died, and she settled back into her chair.

"I'm debating walling it off again from the main house to keep them out," Ian continued.

Lara gasped. "Oh, they'll be heartbroken."

"Temporarily. I can't have them running around in there, chasing ghosts."

She straightened as a chill raced down her spine. "Ghosts? Who said anything about ghosts? I thought they were after a mouse."

Ian snorted. "Is that what made you ask Rollo about mice earlier today?"

She nodded. "Friday, when the twins went running into the old wing…yes, against your orders and mine…I heard them yelling 'there he is.' I made them get out but forgot to ask them what they were after." She gestured toward the hallway. "They came out covered in dust."

"Hmmm. I didn't see any sign of rodent droppings or damage."

"They must have been chasing Scamp. You've seen the cat."

"Maybe." Ian set his mug aside and leaned back in his chair.

He wasn't quite sprawled as he had been earlier, but Lara took it as a sign the change of topic had relaxed him.

"You've lived here for more than a year. And you haven't heard any tales about a ghost?"

Was he kidding? "This house is haunted? You can't be serious." She gripped her mug, suddenly wondering if she'd get any sleep tonight. "No, I've never…"

"I don't know about the newer part, but there are old tales of the ghost of the keep—which may refer to the old wing. They're probably just that…tales meant to keep the curious away. But this is Scotland, and the north wing is the original structure on this estate." He gave her an evil grin and waggled his eyebrows. "Hallowe'en is coming. You never know which spirits will walk about that night."

Ian's teasing tone failed to reassure her. Lara gulped, all concerns about the wedding forgotten. Ghost stories had scared her as a kid, and she still would not— could not— watch horror movies. "What should I do?"

Ian gave her a lazy shrug. "Nothing to do. If it wants to show itself, it will. If not, it won't. I doubt it'll come in here."

Lara eyed the hallway leading to the opening Ian had cut. "You gave it a way in."

"I don't think any wall could stop a ghost. No ghost has bothered you yet. If the tale is real, I doubt it will."

"Bother us…how?" A shiver ran down Lara's spine.

"Well, the tales are not clear. I've heard, though, the ghost is a well-behaved sort who will do the laird's bidding, so you've nothing to worry about."

She didn't know whether to laugh or cry at that. Nothing to worry about? "Only there is no laird anymore."

Ian stared off into space and didn't answer.

CHAPTER 5

*I*an knew this would be a good time to come clean with Lara about his connection to Cairn Dubh. She would find out soon enough, and he'd rather she heard it from him. But something held him back. Self-interest, surely. Curiosity, too. He hadn't explored the wing's upper floors yet, or found the hidden room he suspected would fill out the blank space in his floor plan. He wanted to see the rest before she found out who he was and fired him. And, truth be told, he wanted to be the one to preserve the old keep. No one else would do as good a job as he would. No one would care as much about finding any hidden problems. The thought that it could collapse to the ground in his lifetime kept him awake at night. Wouldn't that be a fine legacy?

Worse, what if Lara or the twins got hurt in there? He grimaced at the thought. No, he'd been given the second chance he thought would never come his way. He would keep his mouth shut for as long as he could and make the most of it.

He could feel Lara's gaze on his face as surely as if her palm warmed his cheek. She tapped a finger nervously on the table. She had to be waiting for him to tell her more about the ghost. Too bad there wasn't much more to tell. He didn't know who it was supposed to have been or why it would hang around to haunt the old keep. No one did, not anymore. The origin of the legend was as lost as the ghost.

He met her gaze and smiled. "Maybe there's time to do a little ghost hunting before the twins get home from school. Why don't we go see if we can scare up the auld specter?"

Lara let go of her mug so suddenly, it tipped, then dropped back to the tabletop with a thump. "What? Oh, no you don't." She shuddered slightly. "You'll leave me in the dark, jump out, and scare me half to death. I don't think so."

Ian didn't think she was serious, so he grinned. "Really? You're not the least bit curious about the rest of that wing?"

"Of course I am, but I'll wait for you to string lights up there, thank you very much. We tried exploring by flashlight. That...draft...on the stairs was...God, I can't believe I'm about to say this: spooky."

Ian recalled wondering if she was afraid of the dark. Could the darkness, and not the idea of a ghost, as she seemed to want him to believe, be making her nervous? He reached for her hand, then thought better of it. He was trying to put her at ease. Teasing her, not seducing her. Or maybe seducing her by teasing her. Christ, he'd better not screw this up. "Where's your sense of adventure, lass?"

She eyed him. The glance she gave his hand told him she'd noticed his aborted movement. "Safely stored away under lock and key. Just trying to live in Scotland turns out to have been more than enough adventure for me. I don't need to annoy the resident ghost, too. If there is one."

Ian shrugged, ashamed he'd inadvertently raised the specter of Angus, whose sudden passing had most certainly ruined the adventure of moving here. She'd had a tough go of it, no question. "It's just a story," he assured her. Maybe.

"One I was quite happy to remain ignorant of. If I'm jumping at shadows from now on, it'll be thanks to you." She crossed her arms and looked again toward the hallway. "It's bad enough the twins are running around the place chasing—and I can't believe I now hope for this—a mouse. I'll be happy if it's only a mouse."

"Like as not."

"You can say that. You're not out here alone during the long dark nights…" Lara colored and trailed off.

Ian's body responded, tightening enough he was glad the table separated them. Actually, he wasn't glad at all. If he wanted to use the perfect opening she'd just given him, all he had to do was take her in his arms and let things go from there. She couldn't mistake how he'd interpret her words any more than he could mistake her embarrassment when she realized what she'd implied. But nay, it was too soon. He took a breath and forced himself to pretend his mind hadn't gone where hers obviously had. As much as he knew he'd enjoy spending the long dark nights here in her bed, he'd be wise to take his cue from her hesitation. Cairn Dubh was miles from the lights of town and much darker once the sun went down. The contrast with where she came from in California must be even more dramatic. With only the twins for company, and without a man for comfort and protection…ach, weren't his thoughts heading in a very medieval direction? This place was getting to him, too.

He stood and stretched out a hand. "Come on. It's time to shed some light in dark corners. All this talk has pushed my buttons. I've got lots of torches. Let's explore. Then you won't need to be nervous about what you've never seen. You'll know what's there."

To his great surprise, she rose. "I'm not sure. Though, honestly, I'm curious, too. If you think it's safe."

"We'll be careful."

~

A few minutes later, Rollo greeted them as they entered the old wing's ground floor. He took one look at the torches in their hands and nodded. "Going to have another look around? She's sound enough unless the roof has leaked onto the top floor. Watch where ye put your feet."

Ian nodded. "We'll do that." He waved Lara to his side. "Let's keep your light in reserve," he said. "I want you to stick close to me."

She rolled her eyes at him. "Is that supposed to reassure

me? Because it didn't work." She didn't wait for him but started walking forward.

Ian chuckled at her droll comment, flicked on his torch, and followed. He had an app on his phone, too, for more light, but didn't mention it. He wanted her close to him. He certainly didn't want her to wander away from him into danger. He let her lead the way, but only a pace or two ahead of him. On the stairs, he stayed ready to catch her if she should stumble. They entered several first-floor rooms, all empty. When they got to the one Ian suspected fronted a hidden space, he started tapping on the adjacent wall.

"What are you doing?"

Lara's question deserved an answer. He just didn't have a good one yet. "This is where the interior measurements don't line up with the outside dimensions," he told her. "I think there might be something hidden behind this wall."

"Really?"

"Or it might be nothing—just a very thick section of outer wall where it makes a corner with the main house. I'm not hearing anything to suggest a void, but, honestly, I didn't think I would. This is stone, not plaster. Rollo and I will have to drill through the mortar to see if there's a void back there."

"Wow, that's mysterious. Why would they hide a room?"

"For a very good reason, or no reason at all," Ian answered with a distracted smile as he studied the stonework. "Sometimes things get closed off in additional construction —like when they built the newer part of the estate. Restorers have found stairways going nowhere, empty voids in corners, you name it. But in some of Scotland's history, having a hidden space was useful, even crucial to survival. Say, if you happened to be a priest during the Reformation."

"I had no idea."

"Let's go up one level and see if there's a wall in the same place."

"If you think it's safe."

"New territory from here on," he intoned, unable to resist playing to the mood of the place. His torch's beam did a decent job of exposing the empty space around them as they made their way to the next set of stairs.

Lara's shoulders lifted when they reached it as she sucked in a breath. She flicked on her light, exhaled and nodded. "Let's do this."

"Remember, the stone isn't level. Take your time and watch where you put your feet." He wouldn't mind holding her in his arms again, but he'd rather not risk a fall up here in the dark. "In fact, I'll go first. You can hold onto my shoulder."

"No, I can do it." She scowled at the steps, and her chin jutted stubbornly toward them, then she started up.

"Brave lass." Ian followed on her heels. She kept her light focused on the stone steps at her feet. He used a steady rhythm to sweep the bright beam of his torch in a narrow side-to-side arc, illuminating the next several steps, and checking their joints at the walls while he was at it. No gaps. So far, so good.

They reached the landing for the next level without incident, and Lara surprised Ian when she killed her light without him asking her to. He played his light around as they explored, seeing what he expected to find—another empty level—then swept the beam across the floor, estimating measurements with an expert eye. "This wall runs just above the one I want to drill into downstairs," he muttered, more to himself than to Lara. "Wait here a second, lass." He paused while she flicked on her light before he walked back to the stairs then down a few steps and hollered, "Rollo, can ye hear me?"

"Aye." The answer came from the level below, nearby.

"I need a drill with a mortar bit and the snake camera."

"Aye. Give me a minute."

Ian went back down the hall to Lara, who waited calmly enough, playing her light over the ceiling and into nearby rooms. He let his tread get louder on the bare wooden floor so he wouldn't startle her. "Empty?" he asked as he approached.

"As far as I can see. I didn't want to move around too much without you."

"Good lass. Rollo will be up in a minute with some equipment…"

"I heard you. Why do you want to drill up here instead of downstairs?"

"The wall may be thinner here than below. Faster to punch through, if we're lucky."

"Here I am," Rollo interjected from the top of the stairs, torch beam preceding him. "Let's see what's caught your eye." He handed the snake cam to Ian before stepping up to the wall.

Ian indicated a seam in the mortar about chest high, a

convenient level to stand and steady the drill, and pointed his light toward it. If there was a void back there, the camera could get a good view toward the floor, where odds and ends tended to collect. Lara moved to Rollo's other side and added her light to Ian's. Rollo placed the bit and pulled the trigger. No one tried to speak over the noise while the drill chewed through the mortar. Before long, Rollo reversed the spin and pulled the drill bit free. Ian turned on the camera and threaded its cable through the hole, then grabbed his mobile out of his back pocket and opened the camera's app. What he saw took his breath away.

~

*L*ara held her breath when Ian's eyes went wide. "What is it?" she demanded, curiosity fully piqued. Ian passed her his phone, and she frowned at the image. The camera's high intensity light revealed a staircase, and propped against the adjoining walls, boxes or chests and other things she couldn't immediately identify. She gave Ian a puzzled glance and handed the phone to Rollo.

"Well, it appears we have more demolition to do," Rollo remarked. "Very carefully."

"Here and on the floors above and below, as well, or I miss my guess," Ian responded. "They walled off around that staircase for a reason."

"What do you think those things are? Besides the stairs, I mean," Lara asked.

Ian shrugged. "We won't know until we get inside this wall." He put a hand flat on the stonework. "Not a priest's hole, I think. Not here. This level looks like storage—it's pretty big as hidden rooms go. Rollo, see if you can move the camera around."

Rollo handed the phone back to Ian and slowly twisted the thin cable protruding from the wall. Ian held the phone where they all could see it.

Glimpses of what lay beyond the landing left Lara stunned. Ian didn't say a word while Rollo kept the arc of light moving ever higher, then down and to the side. If there was an opening for stairs leading down, it wasn't visible behind what appeared to be beautiful, if somewhat dusty, wooden and upholstered furniture, paintings and tapestries hanging on whitewashed walls, sconces, candelabra, knickknacks on small tables tucked wherever they'd fit. She couldn't take it all in, but what she could see must have been worth a fortune, once upon a time. Whoever hid all this away had to have been prominent and wealthy. Even Ian seemed overwhelmed, his eyes wide and his breathing more rapid than she'd ever noted before.

"We need a sledgehammer," Ian muttered. "A hammer and chisel at least, to start taking down these stones."

Rollo nodded. "I'll bring both. Do ye want some men to help with this?"

Ian surprised her by shaking his head. "Nay. Let's keep this among we three until we know what we're dealing with."

Rollo nodded, grabbed his flashlight out of his back pocket, and headed down the hallway to the stairs.

"How are you going to get this wall down?"

"Carefully. We won't take all of it. Just enough to let us get in there. I don't want it to collapse and destroy whatever has been preserved behind it all these years. I do want to know if the stairs have been blocked off, or if we can use them to get to the ground floor and above this level without breaking through the walls on those levels."

"Can we see anything else with the camera?"

Ian watched the display on his phone while he twisted the cable. "Not much. But it shouldn't take long to get a few of these stones out of the way, and then we'll have a much better view."

Lara was impressed by how quickly Ian and Rollo made a hole in the wall while taking obvious care not to allow any debris to fall into the hidden space. Removing the first stone was hardest. Once they had a few more out of the way, the work went faster. They didn't pause to study what they revealed. They only stopped to discuss whether the upper part of the wall would stay put above what they cleared. They seemed determined to make the space big enough to enable them to actually enter the hidden room. Finally, when they stopped altogether, Lara could step right in. Ian would have to duck. Rollo, too. "Is there room for all of us?"

"Let's get a closer look," Ian suggested and moved deliberately forward, playing a beam of light over the floor ahead of him. He stepped over the low barrier they'd left in place and ducked through.

Lara flicked on her flashlight and followed. Here and there, silver gleamed and crystal flashed, reflecting the first light directed at it in years. From the look of these furnishings, a hundred years, maybe two, she thought. "Why would someone leave behind so many beautiful and probably, even in their time, valuable things? And seal them away?" She waved both hands in a wide arc, encompassing the room. She guessed it was easily fifteen feet long, if only six or seven feet wide. The far corners were lost in gloom, outside the flashlight's glow unless she pointed the beam that way.

Ian's expression, just visible in the reflected flashlight gleam, looked grim, his lips compressed into a thin line. "Perhaps they meant to come back. Something happened to prevent them, and the new owners never knew this was here."

"That's so sad."

Ian swept the beam along the furniture and tabletops. "This area has been sealed off for a very long time. Still, I'm shocked no one has suspected its existence, broken in, and pilfered it." He played his flashlight beam up the walls.

A large painting of a Scottish deerhound in an ornate frame dominated the wall fronting the staircase.

"Look at him," Lara breathed and moved closer, threading her way between chairs and side tables to reach the outside wall. "What a beautiful painting. Someone must have loved that dog."

"Aye, I expect so." Ian brought the light closer.

Something glinted at the bottom of the frame. Lara rubbed away the dust to reveal an engraved brass plate. "It says 'The Macaulay's Finest, Fergus.' Do you suppose that's the dog's name?"

"I have no idea." Ian played the light over the painting. "He must have been a damn fine hunting dog for them to immortalize him this way."

"He looks fierce enough." Lara studied the brass plate again. "Who was the Macaulay?"

"Is there a date?"

Ian's question drew her back to the brass plate. "I don't see one. Shine the light in the bottom corners. Maybe the artist signed and dated the painting."

He complied, but even with both lights, she couldn't make anything out. "The artist—or time—has darkened the edges of the image so much, I can't tell. Maybe the date's on the back. We'll see when we get it into better light. Should we take it down?"

"Not yet. Let's look around some more first."

"The stairways are open," Rollo reported. "I'll go down first and see what's below."

"Be careful," Lara told him, earning a grin from Ian.

The other side of the stairway was equally crowded. She had to move carefully to avoid knocking anything over, and her growing excitement made navigating the tight space difficult. "There's too much here," she remarked.

"Aye, some of this must have been stored here from other houses that existed back then."

"Why?"

"Once we figure out what all of this is, maybe it will tell us."

Rollo came back up. "Not much down there." He looked around. "Do ye want to try going up?"

Ian's gaze lifted to the upward stairway. "Might as well. I'll go first, then Lara. You stay here for now in case we get in trouble."

Rollo nodded.

Lara couldn't believe anyone would be content to wait. Her pulse raced with excitement as she followed Ian threading his way toward the bottom of the upward staircase.

Despite their care, by the time they reached it, they were covered in dust from the waist down. She'd track more dust back into the house than the twins had.

She forgot her annoyance at the mess when they reached the top floor. Bedchambers, indeed. This space had been used to store items from the family's private quarters, including beds, bedclothes, washstands, folded lengths of plaid fabric…Lara couldn't take it all in.

"The canopy over this bed appears to be silk," she told Ian, moving closer to get a better view. "And look, the plaid woolens draping the bed look like they have hardly faded through the years. Incredible."

"Ye can thank the deep darkness," Ian answered after a pause that made her tear her attention away from the bed to look at him.

He was staring as if he'd seen a ghost. The ghost? "Are you okay?" she asked. "You seem…"

"I'm fine," he grated out, then cleared his throat. "Let's keep going."

He didn't sound fine, but Lara took him at his word. He wasn't nine years old, and she wasn't his mother.

Everywhere she looked, Lara saw another chest she

itched to open, but Ian suggested waiting until they could see what they were doing.

"No sense damaging the locks, or the contents, if we don't have to," he told her with a noticeable roll to his r's.

She had to agree. "Do you think you could run some lights on these upper levels and break through the wall into this space? Then we wouldn't have to wait until you get the windows opened up."

"Aye. We'll have to, in order to work up here and not damage anything. Much of this has great historical value, I'd guess."

That gave her an uncomfortable jolt. Of course. "Oh dear, is there some sort of historical society we should call to go through all of this?"

Ian frowned and swept the flashlight around the room again. "There is someone we can call for help, but all this belongs to you now."

Lara could have sworn his voice broke at the end of the sentence.

She put a hand on his arm. "You're not all right. The dust is getting to you. I can hear it in your voice. Let's go back down and get cleaned up."

Ian nodded and led her back to the hidden stairs without another word.

He made her follow him down with one hand on his shoulder, something she didn't mind doing at all. She enjoyed his body heat under her hand, the play and flex of his muscles as he moved. Too soon, they reached the bottom, and Lara had to let go. They collected Rollo and filled him in as they made their way out of the hidden room and down the hallway to the main stairs. On the ground floor, Rollo left them. Ian switched off his flashlight and turned to her.

They both heaved a breath at the same time, then she grinned. "Wow," she marveled, at a loss for anything more eloquent to say.

Ian nodded and blinked, his expression serious, even solemn. "Wow."

Were his eyes watering? "Are you allergic to dust?"

"Nay." He rubbed at the corner of one eye with the back of his index finger. "I…well, there's a lot of very old dust up there. So maybe…"

Lara nodded, unconvinced. But why else would his eyes be damp?

CHAPTER 6

The snow had stopped by the time Lara left to pick up the twins. She took her time, driving carefully on the narrow road into the village, mindful of the stone walls lining both sides and the possibility of slick spots that could cause her to slide into them. Snow dusted the pine branches on either side, part of a commercial woodland intended to be harvested every few decades. She would hate to see the trees cut down, but understood they offered little in the way of food or shelter to local wildlife. Once they were gone, the area would be replanted with native plants and hardwood trees to let a healthy forest develop, much like the woodlands on the Cairn Dubh estate. It was another reason she'd come to love the place and wanted to preserve it. Not a day passed when she and the twins didn't see birds, rabbits, and occasionally, deer and other animals unfamiliar to her.

But no ghosts. Other than her concern over Ian's reaction to the dust—if that's what it had been—she'd been thrilled with what they'd discovered. There had been no repeat of the strangely chill breeze they'd felt on the lower floor the first time they'd started up a set of stairs in the old wing. That was reassuring. Surely any ghost worth its…whatever…would have objected to their intrusion into the hidden space, right? So she could relax. There was no ghost.

Lara arrived as school let out. The twins were ready to go and chattered about their day all the way home. She had to bite her tongue to keep from telling them about hers. Hearing what she and Ian had found would only encourage them to explore.

Ian and Rollo were outside when they arrived. At first Lara thought they were ready to leave. Then she noticed boxes marked "Industrial Lighting" on the snow-dusted ground by Rollo's truck. Ian was as good as his word. They'd gotten more lights to run to the upper levels.

The twins escaped from the car before she could order them inside the house. Instead, they made a beeline for Ian and told him—in stereo—about what they'd learned that day. He took it all in stride, squatting down to their level and nodding sagely at each comment they made until she caught up, in time to hear Alex ask Ian to pick them up again—upside down this time.

"Get inside," she ordered in her sternest voice. "You have homework to do before supper."

"Aww, Mom," Amy complained.

"Another time," Ian promised. "Your mother wants you to do something else right now."

Lara could have kissed him for that.

"We want to hear what Ian found in the old wing today," Alex added.

Ian stood and met Lara's gaze over the heads of her children. He shook his head slightly, telling her Alex's comment had been a lucky stab in the dark. Ian hadn't revealed anything. Nor would he. She nodded and fought not to blush. Despite the treasures they'd found today, the picture that instantly filled her mind was of Ian with his arms around her on the stairs—something she would always associate with the old wing.

"You'll hear about it later. Go on. Now."

Amy gave her a mutinous look but went with her brother when he grabbed her hand and tugged.

Lara's shoulders dropped. One more battle averted. "Does she give you a hard time?" Ian asked.

Perceptive of him. "She misses her father. I'm told it'll only get worse in a few years when puberty hits."

Ian's lips quirked. He glanced the way the twins had gone. "Alex seems to do a good job as mediator."

"So far. But don't believe his innocent expression. He gets in trouble right along with his sister."

"I'll keep that in mind."

Rollo had carried the lighting boxes inside while they talked with the twins. Ian took her arm and led her to the door.

She gestured him inside, then closed the door, shutting out the cold, and led the way to the kitchen. "I've been thinking about dust." She gestured toward the hallway to the old wing. "When I thought the twins had chased a mouse…and Scamp…in there, they came out covered in it. I'm afraid all the dust means they went upstairs."

"Not necessarily." Ian shrugged. "The ground level is plenty dirty, especially if they sat on the floor."

Lara nodded, then brushed her hands together as if wiping off dust. "Yeah, I can see them crawling around, looking for a mythical mouse."

"Well, no matter, and no harm done." Ian nodded toward the old wing's opening. "But it's still wise to keep them out of there. Especially away from the upper floors."

"No kidding. Now we've opened the hidden rooms, I don't want them to get in there and break anything." She shuddered, thinking about the damage her two might do to ancient and possibly priceless artifacts.

"Nor do I." Ian frowned, then his expression cleared. "I'll let you get on with whatever you need to do. I expect Rollo is waiting for me to help with the lights."

The twins rocketed into the kitchen just as Ian was about to go.

"What's for dinner, Mom?" Alex asked.

Her growing boy, always hungry. Lara ruffled his hair, then, for good measure, Amy's, too.

Ian paused, watching the twins with a hint of a smile lifting the corner of his mouth.

Lara decided that while he was here, it would be a good time to ask the twins what they'd been up to. "So," she said, keeping her tone light and non-accusatory, "what were you chasing Friday, you two?"

"Chasing? Us?" Alex put on his best innocent

expression, which told her something was decidedly going on.

"You yelled 'There he is' before you went charging into the place you'd been told to stay out of. So who was 'he' and what makes 'him' interesting enough to disobey me—and Ian?"

Alex and Amy exchanged a look. Lara could have sworn Amy looked a little pale. It must be a trick of the lighting.

"Just Scamp," Amy answered, squaring her shoulders. Another bad sign. "We didn't want him to get hurt."

"And I don't want either of ye to get hurt in there," Ian countered, his half smile having been replaced by a frown. He joined the inquisition in full Scots brogue and moved to stand next to Lara. "So ye'll stay out until yer mother and I say ye can go in, or I take ye in. Do ye understand? I mean every word."

Amy bristled. "You're not my father. I don't have to do anything you say."

"Amy MacLaren! Apologize, right now."

Amy balked, eyes wide with disbelief. "You're taking his side?"

Lara narrowed her eyes at her rebellious daughter. "When it involves your safety, absolutely. Now apologize. You're being rude." Amy was stubborn enough now. How was she going to survive her daughter's teen years?

Amy looked like she was going to argue some more, then, after a glance at her brother, dropped her gaze and said, "I'm sorry." But she said it to the room and not directly to Ian.

"Thank you," Ian replied, then caught Lara's eye and shrugged.

"Very well," Lara said, acknowledging Amy's effort at civility and silently blessing Ian for attempting to lay down the law. "No unauthorized exploration or you'll be grounded for the rest of your short life."

Alex had the grace to gulp, but Amy's chin lifted, ready for battle.

"We didn't see anything dangerous," she complained. "Just a couple of big empty rooms."

Lara noted Alex's posture stiffen. Ian cleared his throat.

She nodded permission for him to speak.

"You are not qualified to judge what is dangerous and what is safe, especially in a structure as old as that," Ian told the twins, his expression stern and his brogue mostly gone. "Ye'd best do as your mother says if you want to see any more of that wing…until the restoration is over and done."

Lara almost laughed. He knew. So he could read Alex's body language, too.

Her son's curiosity was killing him, and the idea of missing any part of what might be found in the old wing would keep him in line. "Is there anything else you two want to tell me about your wanderings where you were told not to go?"

Both shook their heads and dropped their gazes to the floor. Something was not being divulged, but she knew they weren't going to fess up, not now. And maybe not until she separated them and gave them the full mommy treatment.

"All right. You know the rules. Go finish your homework. Dinner will be ready in an hour."

They took off running.

Ian watched them go with a twinkle in his eye and a slight smile on his lips. "They're up to something."

"You noticed." Lara turned to him and shrugged, trying not to stare at his mouth. He had a whole repertoire of smiles, but she thought she liked the little, subtle ones the best. "Trust me, they're experts at withstanding interrogation. They won't crack until they're ready."

Ian laughed out loud.

Lara decided then and there she loved his laugh, too. He didn't laugh often. He smiled, he chuckled, but he rarely laughed. She wanted to keep him around until he did it again.

"Would you like to stay for dinner?" She couldn't believe she'd asked him, but after mentioning it to the twins in front of him, it really was the only polite thing to do. "I can't promise how it'll go with the terrible twosome, but if you're game…"

He cocked his head and studied her for a moment, then his smile widened. "After I give Rollo a hand, I'd love to."

~

Ian sipped his whisky and stared into the library's fireplace. The flames were low. In a few minutes, he'd have to get up and add another log. But for now, he was content to enjoy the glow and listen to Lara cajoling her kids to turn out the lights and go to sleep. It all sounded so good. Comforting. Just what this house needed. Dinner had been fun. Despite Amy's earlier outburst, the twins had been well behaved—even chatty. He'd enjoyed watching Lara interact with them over a meal. And he'd been very aware of the number of times her gaze had strayed to him.

Some private time this evening, if he read her signals correctly, would be even better than dinner had been.

Exploring the old wing with her had turned into more than he'd expected. Even his shock and excitement over what they'd found hadn't distracted him from liking her hand on his shoulder coming down the stairs. Holding her in his arms after she'd slipped had made him hungry to hold her again. If his luck held, he might get the chance tonight. He set his glass aside and scrubbed his face with both hands. What was he thinking?

He worked for her. The job she'd hired him to do was important to her, but even more important to him, especially after what he'd seen today. The last thing he needed to do was scare her into firing him. He'd enjoy getting close to her as fast as he possibly could, but taking it slow was a smarter strategy. With the main house nearly done, she didn't need him as much as she had three months ago. Someone else could finish the old wing without inconveniencing the family at all.

To get his mind off of what he'd like to do with Lara, he studied the empty wall above the fireplace. It looked just large enough for the painting they'd found. The Macaulay's Favorite, Fergus, would look right at home up there. Had it once hung there, then been hidden away, along with the other treasures?

He thought back to the strange draft he and Lara had felt on the stairs. If he believed the tales, breaking into the old wing and wandering near the hidden rooms might have disturbed a ghost and freed it from whatever held it in thrall these last two hundred and fifty years. He suspected the twins had seen it Friday evening and chased it back where it came from. The looks on their faces while their mother questioned them had convinced him Scamp was not their quarry. Unless the ghost was real enough to have chased Scamp...possible, but surely the cat would have hissed and spat loud enough for Lara to hear. He didn't want to jump to conclusions, especially this time of the year, when spirits were reputed to walk free, but one conclusion was hard to avoid. Nay, it wasn't Scamp. It wasn't a mouse.

All Hallows Eve would be upon them soon. How convenient to have their very own ghost.

The legend wasn't full of details. Ian wondered when— or if—the ghost would show itself to anyone other than the twins, instead of merely brushing by as he believed it had on the stairs. The more he learned about this place, the more convinced he became that the legend was true.

He picked up his glass and held it up so the firelight glowed in the amber liquid. No specter appeared, outlined in flame and whisky. Just as well. Until one did, there was Lara, a delightful, delectable puzzle. Angus had been gone nearly a year and, though he knew everyone grieved differently, he hoped Lara was ready to move beyond her grief. She'd been thinking about kissing him, there on the stairs, just as he'd been ready to kiss her. But then she'd pulled away and acted so cool, he'd wondered if that heated awareness between them had been all in his imagination.

He hoped what happened on the stairs meant she was beginning to heal. But it also meant he'd have to ignore his body's urges and let her take the lead, both for her sake, and so he could keep this job.

She entered the room so silently he would not have known she was there except he noticed movement out of the corner of his eye. After thinking so hard about the ghost, he jumped, expecting to see some apparition gliding into the room. He covered it by shifting toward her, patting the couch next to him in invitation and smiling.

"I'll just get the whisky while I'm up and top off your glass," she told him with an answering smile.

He stood and watched her move to the whisky table and pick up a bottle, graceful and beautiful, a dream come to life. His dream, and the key to everything he'd ever desired. His grip tightened around his glass as he joined her. He'd thought his dream impossible for so many years, he couldn't believe it might now be attainable. So close, but still just out of reach. He had to take this slowly.

To get his mind off of wanting her, he asked, "How are the twins?"

"Sleeping, I hope." She glanced his way for confirmation the bottle she held was what he was drinking, and after he nodded, she continued, "Chastened by getting a lecture about their weekend adventure. Thank you for setting them straight. I hope they'll listen this time."

"Whether they do or not, they're good bairns, Lara. You should be proud."

She nodded and poured for him, then poured a short dram for herself before clinking her glass with his. "Cheers." She hoisted her glass.

"Sláinte," he replied. As he sipped, he contemplated taking her in his arms. But the feeling he got from her was social, not sensual. He led her back to the couch and sat opposite from where she settled, giving her some room. Lara propped an elbow on the back of the sofa and rested her cheek on her fist, gazing at him. "I am proud. And can I say, amazed? You're so good with them," she said.

"I understand what they're going through." Ian pursed his lips, then told her, "I lost my parents when I was nine."

"Oh, Ian, I'm so sorry."

"It was a long time ago. My grandda raised me, and he was brilliant, but I ken how they feel. He passed a year ago."

She reached over and squeezed his hand. "He did a good job."

It would be so easy to tell her what his grandfather had hoped was here, in this house, but he couldn't bring himself to admit how he'd kept it from her all this time. Not yet. To distract himself, he looked away and studied the fire, turning his whisky glass in his hands.

"So tell me about yourself," Lara prompted, drawing his gaze back to hers. "How did you get into restoring old estates?"

Her hair glinted gold in the firelight. Her light blue eyes took on a greenish cast, a mix of sea and sky. The whisky glossed her lips, making them look plump and kissable. It took more effort than Ian imagined possible to form words and answer her, but he knew her question was meant to help get his mind off of his loss. "I studied history and architecture at university. In summers, I worked for a friend's father. He has a construction company, and there are always plenty of odd jobs for a starving student to do. I learned from him, then struck out on my own." He shrugged. "You'll have noticed we've no lack of old buildings needing repair and restoration."

"I've noticed," she replied with a twist of her lips. "And I appreciate what you've done to Cairn Dubh so far. But won't the old wing be more of a challenge?"

"Not really." He picked up his glass and took a sip, happy the conversation had naturally turned away from him, and so easily, too. Yet, he was still full of the foreboding that plagued him each time he imagined what was to come. When Lara found out about him, and eventually she would have to even if it meant telling her himself, his dream would die. She'd never understand. She'd only see what he'd hoped to gain and think he'd used her, even though that was never his intent. "There is little paneling or plastering to remove from the walls—inside or out. Rollo hasn't found any plumbing or wiring to trace and replace. The structural elements are relatively accessible. Once I'm satisfied all of it is solid, and once we fit new windows into the bricked-up openings, we can build from the outside walls in. What do you think you'll do with all the space? Open a B&B?"

She shrugged. "Honestly, I don't know. I realize what I decide will affect what you do in there. I can't see myself as an innkeeper. The twins have to come first, and over the next few years, they'll be more involved with after-school activities and sports. And moving back to California is always an option. I don't think I want to be tied down taking care of guests."

Ian nearly choked on a sip of whisky. Moving back to California? She'd never mentioned that possibility before. He tensed, not liking the idea one whit. "You could hire someone to run it for you." Better to keep her focused on what her life could be here.

"I suppose. But once the restoration is done, selling and moving back to the States is something I'll have to consider." Her gaze settled on the hearth, a frown line between her brows.

Damn, he didn't like hearing her talk about leaving. And he hadn't brought up her plans to add to her problems, but to steer the conversation away from him. "You don't need to decide tonight."

"I know. I'll think about it." She took another sip of her whisky and cocked her head. "So what do you do when you're not running a restoration?"

Ian kept his expression neutral and racked his brain to find another topic to divert her. "All the normal things. Laundry, grocery shopping."

"Do you go out with friends?"

"Of course."

Scamp suddenly dashed past the open library door, his tread thumping as loudly as a running cat's could, racing down the hall toward the kitchen.

"He can be fast when he wants to be," Lara said and

chuckled, her gaze toward the now-empty hallway. "But it always amazes me how much noise one cat can make."

Ian nodded, but he wondered. Was it only the cat?

~

*L*ara tucked her legs up onto the couch and sipped her whisky. Talking with Ian, sharing a drink in front of the fire, made her feel more cozy and comfortable than she'd been in months. She felt honored that he'd finally shared more about his past with her and sad for his losses, but glad that they made him empathize with the twins. There was a lot to like about Ian Paterson.

And a lot of reasons to keep her distance, she reminded herself. The renovation. The option of returning to California. The anniversary...even the twins, despite how well they got along with him. *Off limits.*

She frowned at the fire.

"What's amiss?" he asked, running his fingers up her arm to cup the fist where she'd propped her head.

A line of fire trailed under his fingers, and she fought to keep from nuzzling her face against his hand. "Nothing, really."

"Then why the frown?"

She tore her gaze from the hearth and met his. Nothing in his expression gave her any indication of anything other than care and concern. It lacked the heat his touch had shot through her, making her hope she might see desire reflected in his eyes.

"It's just that this is going to be a difficult week," she

answered, taking her cue from him. "It's been a rough year…I'm not sure how to handle the anniversary. The twins…"

He squeezed her hand, then let go and moved his to the back of the couch. "I think you'll be surprised at how resilient they are. Even Amy. With school and the restoration work in the old wing to distract them, the anniversary will be here and gone before they know it." He paused, then added, "I'm more concerned about you."

She lifted her head. "That's sweet of you, but you needn't worry. I'll be fine. I think I'm dreading this more for the twins' sake than mine."

"I hope that's all it is. And I know how to keep you busy. Once we get lights installed upstairs, you'll want to examine and catalog everything in those rooms." He crossed his arms. "I have a friend who's an antiquities appraiser. I've known her for years and respect her expertise. I can guarantee she'll be discreet. And she can help you decide what to keep and what to sell or donate, either to a museum or to a charity. Let her do the preliminary, and then when you're ready for the word to get out, you can hire someone else to go through everything again and give you another opinion."

"That sounds like just what I need. Thank you."

Ian nodded and tossed off the last swallow of his whisky. "I'd best be going," he said, set the glass aside, and stood.

Disappointed, Lara stood, too. Did she want him to stay? Enough to try seducing him? Lord, she was years out of practice. The idea of throwing herself at Ian terrified her. Allowing him to turn her body into his arms on the stairs was one thing. Making the first move here and now was quite another. *Off limits.* It made her angry. She should be able to enjoy him, if she wanted to. If he wanted to, as well. "If you think you should…" she finally replied, hoping he'd change his mind.

"I'll call Caitlin first thing in the morning and make arrangements for her to come out."

Lara walked with him to the front door. "I'm looking forward to meeting her. I'm sure going through the contents of those hidden rooms with an expert will be fascinating."

Ian gave her one of his rare smiles. "Sleep well. I'll pick you up in plenty of time to get to the elopement."

Good grief, she'd almost forgotten. And she had yet to figure out what to wear. Well, whatever she had would have to do. She had no time to shop for a new dress. "I'll be ready," she promised.

Ian nodded and looked, for one blazing moment, like he would reach for her. He tensed and his gaze dropped to her mouth. But he didn't follow through. He pursed his lips and nodded again. "I know you will."

With that, he slipped out, closing the door behind him. Lara leaned her back against it, seeing nothing but Ian. What had run through his mind, there at the end? Did he want to kiss her? If so, his control was remarkable, and as frustrating to her as it must be to him. He hadn't said much, but the fact that he'd tensed when she mentioned selling Cairn Dubh and returning to California gave her hope. Once the restoration was done, he shouldn't care who owned the place. Could it be he didn't want her to go? Given the connection that seemed to be developing between them, she hoped so. The longer she knew him, the more she wanted to get close to him, even intimately, but she knew better than to rush into anything physical.

However, she was getting better at reading his moods. And he'd seemed uncomfortable again when the conversation turned to hiring an appraiser. Was this Caitlin really just a friend? Or something more? Well, she didn't have to use the woman. Surely there were others she could find if she didn't suit, or seemed dishonest. Or worse, was sleeping with Ian.

Ian appreciated Lara's promptness. None of this feminine messing about for fifteen or thirty minutes while he stared at a wall or paced. When he arrived, she was ready and waiting for him, which given how eager he was to see her again, suited him fine.

"Good morning," he said as she stepped out of her door. She wore a blue dress that fit her curves nicely, front and back, which he got to see when she turned to lock the door. Definitely coming out of mourning, he decided happily. And taking her to a wedding should help move that process along, if it didn't make her maudlin, recalling her own wedding to Angus. He'd do what he could to prevent that, including delivering lame compliments that didn't begin to express how she captivated him. He took her hand as she turned back to him. "You look lovely."

Lara grinned, looking him up and down. "You do, too," she answered, then waved her free hand between them. "Look handsome, I mean. Not lovely."

He laughed and walked her to the car, wondering if she thought "lovely" fit because he was wearing a kilt. Not a skirt, which he was sure she knew. Tongue in cheek humor from her, perhaps? "Well, it's not every day you get to see a friend elope in defiance of both sets of families. I thought such an occasion worth the formality of the full kit." Especially since yesterday's dusting of snow was gone and the day promised to be warm enough to wear it properly. He handed her into the car, then went around and climbed in, careful to make sure the kilt covered everything to his knees.

As he drove to town, he noticed her gaze fall on his lap several times. Checking him out? He liked that. If Lara fancied men in kilts, he'd have to find some excuses to wear his more often.

Blane and Cassie were standing outside the registrar's office when they arrived.

Blane shook his hand and smiled. "Thank ye, Baron." His expression changed quickly, his eyes widening in dismay.

Ian kept his flash of annoyance away from Lara. He was certain she hadn't missed the title. He didn't want to see the question in her eyes. He knew the time to answer for his silence would come sooner than he was ready for.

He also spared Blane. It was his wedding day after all. Instead, he took both of Cassie's hands in his and leaned forward to kiss her cheek. "I don't know if it's fair to kiss the bride before the ceremony, but I don't care," he told her with a smile as he let her go. "You're too beautiful to resist."

Cassie tittered and glanced at her husband-to-be, then lowered her gaze.

For a second, Ian feared she was about to curtsey. "I'd like to introduce you to Lara MacLaren," he continued. He turned to her and offered his hand to pull her forward.

"It's lovely to meet you both," Lara said as she slipped her hand into his.

Her gaze was on the happy couple, but she traced her fingertips across his palm, shooting fire along his veins. It took all of Ian's willpower not to react.

"Thank you for inviting me," Lara added smoothly.

Ian nearly growled. The minx knew what her touch had done to him.

"We're pleased you could join us," Cassie offered, then quickly added with an embarrassed twitch of her shoulder. "Or we'd be short a witness."

Lara laughed. "I understand. Ian told me. You're very brave to do this. Families can be so…"

"Difficult?" Blane supplied.

Ian arched a brow at him. Blane had chosen to do this. Was he having second thoughts?

"So, do you have everything?" Lara asked Cassie. "Something old, something new…"

"There was no time," Cassie replied, paling just a bit. She lifted her hand to her earlobe. "The pearls are old, the dress is new, but the borrowed and the blue…"

"I have the perfect thing," Lara told her, pulled her hand from Ian's and unwrapped her blue-floral silk scarf from around her throat. "It'll be borrowed, and it's blue," she added and pressed the scarf into Cassie's hand.

Ian appreciated the kindness of the gesture, but mostly, if he couldn't hold her hand, he was happy to see the milky skin of Lara's elegantly long throat bared. "Oh!" Cassie teared up, her eyes glinting. "Thank you so much!"

"It's nothing," Lara told her, squeezing her hand. Then taking the scarf, she draped it around Cassie's neck, twisting it and tying a knot that left it looking like it belonged with the dress from the beginning.

The architect in Ian was impressed.

"Shall we go in?" Blane glanced at his watch.

Ian nodded and gestured for them to precede him. He'd enjoy following Lara into the hall and the view it would afford him.

Ian tuned out while the registrar went through his welcome speech and started the short ceremony. Standing beside Lara, he could only watch her out of the corner of his eye. The registrar droned on, his pauses punctuated by Cassie's or Blane's responses. Lara watched them calmly until the registrar called for the exchange of rings.

First Cassie slipped a white gold band onto Blane's hand, then Blane did the same for his bride. Their eyes shone.

They looked so hopeful, and so happy, Ian's throat started to tighten. Then he noticed Lara twisting the wedding ring on her left hand. Suddenly, she pulled it off and dropped it into her handbag. Ian's breath froze in his chest. If he hadn't been watching her, he never would have noticed.

She glanced up and gave him a hesitant smile. Did she

know he'd seen what she'd done? Why had she chosen this time and place to take off her ring? Though it wasn't really any of his business, the need to know burned in his belly.

He hoped she'd done it to show him she was ready to move on. Her touch on his palm hadn't been an accident. But this was certainly not the place or the time to find out. As if to emphasize that point, the registrar cleared his throat, distracting Ian.

"Ye are now married," the registrar announced to Blane and Cassie, "and are husband and wife for as long as ye live." He broke his official seriousness long enough to grin at Blane. "Ye may kiss the bride."

Ian forced his attention to stay on his friends as they kissed. Blane shook the registrar's hand as Cassie turned and hugged Ian, then Lara. Then it was Blane's turn. A spurt of jealousy surprised Ian as Blane kissed Lara on the cheek.

"Thank you, again, for standing with us," Blane told her. "I ken we're strangers…"

"Not anymore," Cassie interrupted. "Not after this. Here," she added, untying the knotted scarf, "I should give this back to you."

Lara wiped away a tear. "Of course, you're right. Since it's borrowed, I'll take it." She took the scarf from Cassie's hands, then smiled. "I'm so happy for you," she added and looped it back around Cassie's neck. "Now you're married, it no longer needs to be 'borrowed,' so keep it. It's only a token, but it's my gift to you, to remember this day."

Cassie gasped.

"If you newlyweds will sign the Marriage Schedule, we'll be finished," the registrar broke in.

"Of course," Blane answered.

Ian was happy he pulled Cassie away before she could tear up again. He touched Lara's shoulder. "That was a lovely thing you did. Are you all right? I didn't mean for this to upset you, or I would have tried to find someone else to bring."

Her lips twitched—not quite into a smile. "I'm fine. Weddings always make me cry. It's a family trait." If he'd believed her, Ian would have been relieved.

But she'd taken off her wedding ring. The ceremony had meant something to her, something profound. He took her hands and ran his thumb over her finger where the ring used to be. He didn't say a word, just kept his gaze on her face, on her eyes.

She nodded and her chin quivered, just a bit. "Memories?" he asked.

"Yes." Her gaze dropped, then returned to him. "And the realization…it's time to put them away."

Her words stunned him. She'd just given him permission to pursue her. Relief and anticipation made him pull in a deep breath. "You don't have to forget him," he told her, striving to hide the elation coursing through him.

"I know. And I never will." She closed her eyes and her voice softened. "I see his face, his mannerisms, his way of speaking every day…in the twins." She lifted her gaze to his face. "But he's gone, and I'm here."

"I'm here, too." Three simple words. Not the ones every woman wanted to hear. Plainly she wasn't ready for those, and Ian wasn't ready to say them. But her wide-eyed glance told him she'd heard and understood what he meant.

"I...know. And I'm...grateful."

Grateful? He wanted much more than grateful. He wanted her hungry and eager and making room in her life...for him. He kissed her hands and let them go, biting down on the words he wanted to say. Not the time. Not the place.

~

They finished lunch early, so Ian rang Caitlin to meet them at the house instead of coming out later after Lara retrieved the twins. Caitlin was due any minute. While Lara ran upstairs to change, Ian took advantage of her absence to strip out of the wedding finery and pull on the work clothes he'd carried into the house from the boot of his car. He'd worn the kilt the traditional way, so he was stuck going commando under his jeans. Not the first time—or the last, no doubt. Normally, he wouldn't mind, but the jeans were ice cold, damn it, from spending the morning in the boot. He pulled a long-sleeved T-shirt over his head and followed it as fast as he could with his sweater, hoping that would warm him—all of him. Socks and boots, followed by a full minute of running in place, finally did the trick.

A few minutes later, he stepped outside to put his

wedding finery in his car in time to see Caitlin turn her estate wagon into the lane leading to Cairn Dubh and park behind Ian's car.

"Baron! How wonderful to see you."

"You, too, lass. But don't call me that, no' here." Ian froze at the sound of footsteps coming up behind him on the gravel fronting the house. Lara joined them as he issued the warning. Had she heard? She hadn't said anything after the ceremony yesterday, so maybe she had missed Blane's slip after all.

"Good afternoon, I'm Lara MacLaren." She offered her hand to Caitlin.

She'd changed into jeans and a cream sweater that looked softer than a cloud and hugged her curves in a way Ian approved. And her ring finger was still bare, so she hadn't reconsidered the impulse that led her to remove it during the ceremony. He liked that even more.

"Caitlin Paterson. I'm pleased to meet you, and eager to get to work." Caitlin shook Lara's hand and turned back to Ian. "You gave me a bare-bones description and said you've had time to get lights installed. Shall we have a look?"

Ian turned to Lara. "Are you ready?"

"And eager." Lara led them into the house and through to the old wing, pointing out to Caitlin the work Ian had done as they went. "So, are you two related?" Lara asked as she preceded them up the now brightly lit main stairs.

"Cousins," Caitlin answered. "We grew up in different villages, both nearby."

Ian held his breath. He'd filled her in on the situation

here. He hoped she'd be as discreet with his secrets as he'd promised Lara she'd be about the contents of the hidden rooms. If they'd been sealed for the reason he suspected, those items on the upper floors were of great historical value, and not just to the Macaulays.

"I'll enjoy talking to you, then," Lara replied with a smile over her shoulder at Caitlin. "You can fill me in. Ian's been exceptionally quiet about himself. I learned only a little more about him this morning at the wedding."

Caitlin cast a wide-eyed glance Ian's way. "Wedding?"

"Aye," Ian answered, enjoying Caitlin's shocked expression as she glanced from him to Lara and back again, totally misunderstanding and jumping to a wild conclusion. "Blane and Cassie eloped. We stood with them." And seeing Lara remove her ring during the ceremony had hit him hard. He'd wanted to get her thinking about the start of a new relationship with him, not the end of her marriage with Angus. But perhaps taking off her ring meant she'd done both.

"Ye two?" Caitlin gave them a long look.

"I took pictures." Ian responded, irritated he needed to justify his actions to his cousin. Or anyone else.

"After I thought of it," Lara chided. "They wouldn't have had any to remember the day—or to show their families."

"Assuming they're speaking, now they've defied both, and the deed is done," Ian added. Along with smiles at the newly married couple, he'd seen some frowns cast his way as they left the registrar's office. Whether they were meant to disapprove of his support for Blane and Cassie, or because Lara was with him, he didn't know. But they'd reinforced his reluctance to be seen as taking advantage of her.

"Well, perhaps having family around will make Ian more willing to open up," Lara mused, apparently happy for another chance to needle him.

Inwardly, Ian cringed. If he didn't find the right time to tell her about his possible connection to her estate, the fantasy running in his mind of how good it could be to have her on his arm every day—and in his bed every night —would never come true.

"I'm not sure I'll be much help," Caitlin answered hesitantly, with a glance at her cousin.

Ian planted his fists on his hips. "I am right here, lassies. I can hear you."

"Good."

Ian almost laughed out loud at Lara's curt reply. Her curiosity about him must have been killing her for weeks. He'd managed to keep the lunchtime conversation yesterday focused on the happy couple. Although Caitlin had argued on the phone the sooner he was honest with Lara, the easier it would be to accomplish his goals, he couldn't accept her advice. Not when hearts were involved. Hers and his. Nay, he had to keep playing this close to his chest, and make sure Caitlin didn't ruin everything.

Suddenly he doubted the wisdom of his decision to include his cousin. If she and Lara bonded, well, there was no telling where girl talk would lead them.

They went all the way to the top floor first. Caitlin let

out a whistle, then did a cursory walk through, but made no comment other than to say, "Let's look downstairs."

Lara frowned but led the way to the lower floor and stood by as Caitlin repeated her survey of the upper room, not pausing to look closely at anything—even Fergus's painting.

Ian wanted to bounce on his heels, but he contented himself with shoving his hands into his pockets and balling them into fists. Caitlin's theater would not help keep Lara from overreacting, not if this hoard was what he suspected.

Finally, Caitlin joined them in the hallway area just outside the remaining stone partition and crossed her arms. "I will need to take some time up here," she said to Lara. Then she looked to Ian. "Several items may help me date when these rooms were sealed, if not the reason why." She shrugged and returned her attention to Lara. "And of course, I'll need to do a thorough inventory, photography, the works, before I can give you an estimate with any accuracy. And because there are so many items to be catalogued, this could take a month or more."

Lara frowned. "A month? Really?"

"Or more. Aye. I'll use the inventory and photographs to create a catalog. I must do a great deal of research to verify the provenance of each item."

"But…" Lara turned her gaze to Ian. "What will that do to your schedule for restoring this wing? If all this needs to be removed…"

He shrugged. "'Tis best to wait. Caitlin knows what she's doing."

Caitlin gave Lara a brief, professional smile. "I'm sorry

if you thought this would be a quick process, but to do a good job, and to do the history of these items justice, I must take care."

That was his Caitlin! Ian wanted to cheer. She would buy him all the time he would need, both to woo Lara, and to prepare her for who he really was.

"Will you be able to handle all of this yourself?" Lara asked. "What you described sounds like a lot of work."

"For the most part, yes. I may need to call in a few experts to verify my findings."

"That sounds expensive…"

"Not in the long run. Antiquities auctions depend on trust and verification in establishing value. What's your American saying? You must spend money to make money. But I will, of course, get your approval before doing anything carrying a significant expense."

"Well, that's a relief," Lara muttered to the floor.

Ian quirked an eyebrow and exchanged a quick grin with Caitlin.

"If any of these things have the monetary or historical value I think they have, you will want to hire another appraiser to give you a second opinion. I'm good at what I do, and my findings will be as accurate as I can make them, but I want you to be confident in the identification and valuation of every item."

"You can trust her," Ian interjected. "And the inventory must be done and this space cleared before I can do much in here. Better no' to have a lot of workmen snooping around up here, aye?"

"Until we know what we're dealing with," Lara agreed.

She turned to Ian and added, "Here's another American saying—job security." Then she lifted her chin and gave Caitlin a bright smile. "Where do you want to start?"

~

Lara wasn't unhappy when Ian left them with the promise to check on them later. He said he and Rollo still had plenty to do downstairs, and he needed to take care of some things at his office. Lara hoped if he wasn't around, she might get more information from Caitlin.

Cousins! Lara could barely hide her relief. She didn't need to worry about Caitlin's and Ian's relationship being intimate. And knowing they were related, she could see the resemblance. Caitlin had the same shaped face, the same nose, but her eyes and hair were darker, her build slighter than Ian's.

One thing still bothered Lara—as she joined them outside, had she heard Caitlin call him Baron? She was sure there must be a story to go with the nickname, but she didn't think she'd get it from Ian. Lara could swear she'd heard him hiss at Caitlin not to call him that. It had to be what Becky had started to call him the other day in town.

She'd heard the odd nickname somewhere else, too. Blane greeting him as Baron had slipped her mind in the excitement of the elopement and Ian's declaration after she'd removed her ring. It came back now, along with the emotional turmoil that had swamped her as Blane and Cassie said their vows. She rubbed the part of her finger her ring used to encircle and thought about Ian's words. *I'm here, too.* His eyes had been full of promise…and compassion…and hunger. For her.

But that moment was long past. She'd seen nothing like those emotions from Ian this afternoon. He must have been under the influence of the wedding. Now, he was back to reality, to the friendly but politely and carefully distant self she'd become accustomed to the past few months. She'd always heard weddings did strange things to men…and women. Now she'd seen the proof.

Irritated, she turned to Caitlin. She and Ian's cousin had a lot of work to do.

Not talking must be a Paterson family trait. Once Caitlin finished explaining to Lara how she planned to document the contents of the secret rooms, she had little else to say. Lara settled in a corner and watched as Caitlin moved around, picking up, examining, and replacing some items, like the lace draped over the back of an overstuffed chair, ignoring others, like the swords and dirks piled in one corner. Finally, Lara stood. "Is there anything I can do to help you?"

Caitlin paused and glanced her way. "No thanks. I'm merely doing another cursory look, then I'll fetch my camera and notepad from my car to start the inventory in earnest. I'm used to working alone, so if you have something else you need to be doing…"

Lara shook her head. "Not at the moment. But I have to leave at three to pick up the twins."

"Twins!" Caitlin laid a hand over her heart. "Ian didn't mention you had twins. How old are they?"

Lara chuckled. "Old enough to get into trouble in here. Nine. And a half."

"My, yes." Caitlin nodded. "I look forward to meeting them. Best you keep them occupied somewhere else, though. There are a lot of breakables in here. Some, like that French vase, could be quite valuable."

"I'll do my best, but they are very curious about this wing. Once they see all this…"

"I get it." Caitlin waved a hand in a short arc. "But you must understand what you have here. All this has been locked away for centuries—"

Lara's breath caught. "Do you know how old…?"

"Not yet, but I will. My point is, these items have been untouched for a very long time. And it's not just the individual items, but the collection as a whole, and what it might represent. A window into a time not our own."

"Wow. You really love your work."

Caitlin smiled and glanced around her. "I do. So does Ian. You couldn't have a better man restoring Cairn Dubh. He'll do what's necessary to make it safe and sound, but he'll respect it for what it is and for its history while he does."

Lara ran her fingertips across the back of a wooden chair. "I believe you. I've seen his work the last few months in the main manor. And in here," she said and gestured to take in the entire wing, "he and Rollo are being meticulous about inspecting the foundation."

"I expect so." Caitlin joined her by the chair and gestured for Lara to precede her out of the room. "Look," she added as they moved into the hallway, "I'm ready to start taking pictures. Actually, do you have a camera?"

"What?" The question threw Lara for a second. "I have twins. Of course I have a camera."

"Good. I want you to take pictures, too, of the rooms as a whole and as much as you can get in any one frame at a time while still retaining details. That way, you'll have a record, as well."

Lara frowned. "You don't want to be accused of stealing anything."

Caitlin's head reared back, then she relaxed. "Well, nay, of course not. But I also want you to have a separate record in case anything happens to mine." She waved a hand over the nearby table. "Bar…Ian will be furious if we lose track of any of this." Caitlin swallowed and looked away.

There it was again. Baron. Lara found her patience at an end. "Baron. What does that mean?"

Caitlin shook her head. "Best Ian explain it to you."

"But…"

She held up a hand. "It's no' my place to do."

Lara frowned. "It doesn't seem to be anyone's." She paused, considering how to get Caitlin to spill, then Caitlin's earlier words penetrated. "Why would Ian be furious about losing any of this?"

At the sudden switch in subject, Caitlin frowned in confusion for a moment. "He recommended me," she said.

Her response seemed too glib. Lara crossed her arms and waited.

"He'd see that as harming his reputation, too," Caitlin continued.

That made sense, though Lara still felt Caitlin was holding something back. And like everyone else, she was determined to protect Ian. Lara threw up her hands, conceding defeat for the moment. "Okay. Let's do this."

They went down the stairs together. Lara picked the places to put her feet with care, mindful of the time she slipped in the dark. Not that her near-accident had turned out badly. She'd ended up in Ian's arms, after all, and had nearly kissed him. She shook her head. She'd best keep her mind on her footing, or she'd wind up slipping again on the uneven steps. She didn't think Caitlin big or strong enough to catch her, not the way her cousin had nor the way she wanted him to again.

Lara retrieved her camera while Caitlin went out to her car. She climbed the stairs, alone this time, with even greater care. She was taking pictures on the second floor by the time Caitlin returned with her gear.

"Sorry I took so long. One of my lenses went missing and took a while to find—under a seat, of course. Oh, and Ian's never left. He and Rollo got to comparing notes, I think. He said he'd be up in a wee while to see how we're doing."

Lara's heart skipped a beat, and she turned away to hide her response to Caitlin's news. She really needed to stop reacting every time someone mentioned him. With the camera to her eye and her back to Caitlin she responded, "Good. I'd like to hear how things are going on the ground floor today. The sooner they finish there, the sooner they'll start opening some of these bricked-up windows."

"Oh, not up here," Caitlin objected. "Sunlight will be

bad for the fabrics and papers. We'll work in artificial light until we know what we're dealing with."

Lara frowned and glanced back over her shoulder at Caitlin, who'd moved to photograph some of the items along the far wall. "Ugh. If the lights fail, it'll be dark as a tomb up here."

"You have a torch app on yer phone, aye?"

Ian! She hadn't heard him coming up the stairs.

"Of course we do...cousin," Caitlin's droll response greeted him.

Ian lifted an eyebrow and fastened his gaze on his cousin. Lara guessed he'd not expected her to use that label for him, but she suspected Caitlin had done it deliberately to keep from calling him Baron. Or maybe she meant to apologize for when she called him that, earlier, or to let him know Lara had indeed heard the word before.

Either way, her comment made Lara's curiosity itch. It was odd, and there were enough odd things going on in this house without Caitlin adding to the mix. She and Ian were going to have a chat about this Baron thing—and soon. She'd call him on it now, but Caitlin looked so apologetic when she emphasized the word "cousin", Lara couldn't do it.

"What have you ladies found?" Ian asked, breaking eye contact with his cousin and looking around the room.

"We're just getting started on the photographic record," she told him.

Lara held up her camera to show she, too, was taking pictures.

Ian walked over and stood in front of Fergus's painting,

studying it. "There might be a faint signature in the bottom right corner, but I can't make it out."

Lara joined him and studied the area he'd mentioned. She'd be annoyed with him later. Right now, she could enjoy standing close to him, breathing in his scent and hearing his voice. "No," she told him, "I can't either. Can we take it down and check the back?"

Ian glanced at Caitlin for confirmation, then grinned. "Let's do it."

"Have a care," Caitlin warned as she joined them. "Its frame looks solid, but may not be."

Ian gripped the sides and lifted slightly, testing. "It seems sturdy."

"Okay." Caitlin reached under one of his arms and got a hand around the lower edge of the frame. "Ready? Now."

Lara held her breath as they lifted the painting away from the wall. Behind it, the whitewash was a little whiter, cleaner. That painting had hung there for a long time.

Ian carried Fergus's image closer to one of the overhead lights, then shook his head. "I can't read it."

Lara moved around the painting to get a look at the back. "I see a date! I think it says 1745 in the lower corner. Wow."

Caitlin joined her and photographed the entire back side, then focused her lens on the date. Once satisfied she had a good image, she moved around and photographed the front. "Maybe the signature will be clearer with a different digital filter when I upload the picture to my computer."

"Now you've taken it down, why don't we hang it over the fireplace in the library?" Lara asked.

Ian traded a look with his cousin. "I think old Fergus should stay right here until we know a bit more about what we're dealing with," he told her. "Besides, if someone asks about this painting, how would you explain where it came from?"

Caitlin nodded. "Ian is right. You could make up a story, but if anyone noticed the brass plate on the frame, and they will, you'd be stuck."

"This is an old house. I could have found that painting anywhere—in a closet or an attic. Or I could have bought it at a second-hand shop."

Frowning, Ian shook his head. "Correct me if I'm wrong…cousin…but this painting would carry a very high price in any shop. Likely it belongs in a museum."

Caitlin nodded. "Aye."

"As for a closet or attic, I suppose so, but why only this? What else might be hidden? If you put this on display, you invite questions and possibly even thieves."

"Thieves!" Lara gasped. She would not put the twins at risk. She nodded. "Okay, put him back where he was. There will be plenty of time to find him a new home later."

And why did Ian look so relieved when she agreed?

A cool breeze wafted by Lara's hands, almost like a brush of rough, chilly hair. From Ian and Caitlin's startled expressions a moment later, they felt it, too.

"What was that?" Caitlin exclaimed.

Lara and Ian exchanged a glance and Lara shuddered.

"Not again! That's my cue to leave. I'm going to be late getting the twins."

"I'll walk you out," Ian told her. "Cousin, you'll be all right on your own?"

Caitlin glanced around and shrugged. "As long as whatever that was doesn't come back. You two go ahead. If anything happens, Cousin, I'll scream."

～

"Fergus!" An hour later, Caitlin's exclamation echoed in the open space of the ground floor. "I thought about him a lot after you left."

"Wheesht!" Ian scolded. "Lara or the twins will hear you. I just heard her car on the drive." He dragged her into one of the side rooms, hoping an extra wall would help muffle their conversation. "She's back from picking the twins up from school, and they're in the main house, or will be in a moment."

"But Fergus! The painting! And that weird cold breeze," Caitlin continued, at lower volume. She shivered. "Could the ghost be Fergus?"

"The ghost of a dog?" Ian snorted, then thought about it and shrugged. "Lara says the twins have been up to something ever since I broke through the wall into that wing. They might have seen the ghost...assuming it's real."

"And instead of frightening the twins, the apparition of a dog might seem like something fun. Even friendly," Caitlin argued.

He held up a hand when she made as if ready to go ask them. "But they won't admit to it."

"After seeing that painting, can you doubt it? And what if they go up there and see it? Are they old enough to make the connection?"

"Between the painting and the ghost…if it's a dog? Or if there really is one. I don't know. Anyway, Lara has forbidden them from there. Let's just find some proof first, aye, before we go naming a ghost we're not certain exists." Except for that draft just now and earlier on the stairs… "Speaking of proof, we need to find some dates on the things up there to confirm why these rooms and their stairway were sealed."

Caitlin pointed up. "The plaid on the bed upstairs wasn't enough? They were Jacobites. Had to be. Why else go to such lengths to hide all of the things they valued? To seal all of those things away?"

Ian crossed his arms. "We need a date. Some Jacobite symbols. Provenance is your area of expertise."

"Cairn Dubh is the reason you became an architect in the first place, isn't it? Because you hoped to be the one to restore the estate. To find answers there about your history. Your heritage. If they're here, I'll find them."

"Make sure you do. And don't…" He waved a hand.

"Interpret and create proof? Never." She frowned. "This is too important. And whatever proof I find will have to stand up to scrutiny."

"Exactly."

"But, Ian, you don't own Cairn Dubh. The family hasn't owned it for decades…maybe centuries." Caitlin gasped and backed up a step. "Wait…is that your plan? To reclaim it by marrying the lovely widow? I wouldn't have thought you capable—"

Ian held a hand, palm down. "Shite, Caitlin, keep your voice down. And nay." He shook his head and let his hands fall to his sides. "I'd never do such a thing. No' for that reason, certainly. I have as much right to marry as anyone else, and whether I choose Lara or someone else, taking advantage of a woman will never be part of my decision."

She gave him a skeptical frown, one eyebrow raised.

He curled his hand into a fist and dropped it to his side. How could Caitlin think such a thing of him? "I wouldn't. I like Lara—a lot. But if anything develops between us—"

Caitlin snorted. "Given the looks you two exchange, I think anything is well on the way to developing."

"If…anything develops between us," Ian hissed, "how Lara finds out about…me…will make a big difference in whether it works out." He sighed. "I have to tell her, aye, when the time is right. So, I'll thank you to keep your mouth shut and stick to business. Thank God you suggested she hire a second appraiser. No matter what she thinks of me, at least she won't think you're tempted to pick her pockets."

"Seems to me you'd better tell her soon, before she finds out another way." Caitlin crossed her arms, then waved the top hand. "People talk, and if enough people say a little here, a little there, she'll figure it out on her own. Imagine how that will make her feel."

Ian ran a hand through his hair. "I ken it. She's overheard the title—not only from you. I haven't found the right time to explain. And I don't want her to fire me before I make this building safe for her and the twins. And before you get a chance to figure out what the contents of these hidden rooms mean."

"I think we ken what they mean. Wait, fire you? Do you really expect that to happen?"

Ian gave a resigned shrug. "For her to fire me? Aye. And you right along with me. Wouldn't you, once you knew our connection to this place? I lost the chance to get access and answers a year ago when her husband decided to act as his own general contractor. If he ever knew anything about me, it seems he never told his wife. Now she's a rich widow, and I'm unmarried, so the truth will look even worse to her. I have to convince her I just need to know..."

"We all do, Baron."

He turned and glanced over his shoulder toward the main house. "God, stop calling me that. For all we know the title may never have existed outside of my grandfather's imagination. I know he believed it, and he convinced everyone in the family, the village, hell, the surrounding countryside, but in this century, it's worthless and it could ruin everything."

"Do ye care for her?"

Ian froze, reluctant to admit it out loud. But it was the truth. "Of course I do. She's beautiful and smart and..."

"And for all we ken, she owns your family's ancestral seat in these parts. Your history," Caitlin added and stabbed him in the chest with her index finger. "Yours by right of inheritance, if some prior Baron hadn't supported the wrong side."

He grabbed her hand and pushed it away. "But he did—as far as we can guess—and he lost everything. I may be a successful architect, but I can't afford to keep up this place. Lara can. I'm fine with that."

"Will ye be fine if she marries someone else or decides to sell the place to someone who doesn't care or cannot afford the maintenance? It was on its way to becoming a ruin before MacLaren bought it, and could be again."

"We'll deal with that if it happens, aye? Let's not borrow trouble."

Caitlin pursed her lips and blew out a burst of air. "Nay, let's not. We have trouble aplenty already."

CHAPTER 8

Saturday morning, on the way to the village's market day, Lara could barely contain her emotions. Today was the anniversary of Angus's passing. She hoped the market day would distract the twins and give them something fun to do. As for her…she'd control herself and get through it somehow.

Cairn Dubh had turned out to be so much more than just a home. The contents of the secret rooms would make a wonderful display in a museum, perhaps even in Angus's name. It would be an appropriate way to remember him and to memorialize his connection to the area. The National Museum of Scotland in Edinburgh would probably love to have many of the finer furnishings, art and odds and ends, even weapons, in its collection. If not there, then something in the Highlands, like the visitor's center at Culloden, or even in the village.

If only she could tell someone! But Ian had been clear about the possibility of attracting thieves. He trusted Rollo, but apparently not the men working for him. She would not put the twins in danger, no matter how fitting the idea of donating to a museum in Angus's name seemed today. Ian had appeared quite emotional about what they'd found. He was right. She wouldn't talk to anyone but Ian and Caitlin until arrangements had been made and anything of value removed to safe keeping.

In the backseat, the twins were talking to themselves in low tones Lara knew presaged trouble. "What's going on back there, you two?"

"Nothing, Mom," Alex answered. Lara glanced in the rearview mirror in time to see Amy elbow her brother, then turn her face aside to stare out the window.

"Uh huh. Okay, we're almost there. Remember to stick close to me. I don't want anyone getting lost." She pulled into the car park and found a space. "Ready, lads and lassies? Let's go see what there is to see."

The fairground was filled with small square vendors' tents, and more than a few without cover had their goods piled on tables or on the ground around them in baskets. Alex made a beeline for the ironmonger's display of swords, chain mail and targes, the round shields used by Scottish warriors of old. Amy followed him and fingered the chainmail while Alex drooled over the swords. To keep them out of trouble, Lara had no choice but to go where they went. She didn't need a vendor complaining and getting them kicked out of the market.

"And what's yer name, lad?" the ironmonger asked Alex at the same time Amy called to her.

"Look, Mom, aren't these cool?"

Amy was examining thin belts made out of loosely woven metal loops in many colors—like rainbow chainmail.

"They are colorful," Lara told her just as the ironmonger's voice reached her.

"Aye, I ken the place. 'Tis haunted. Ye would have heard that by now, I expect."

Lara waved Amy to silence so she could hear Alex's response. Would he admit to the man what he and Amy had avoided telling her? But she should have known better —Alex played dumb.

His eyes got wide. "Really?"

"Aye, and a laddie like ye had best keep yer wits about ye. Especially on All Hallow's Eve. The most loyal warrior of the laird guards the old keep still today, armed with a claymore twice yer height and a battle cry to freeze yer blood in yer veins. Ye dinnae want to cross paths with a ghost like that."

Lara pictured a scary man in chain mail with a huge sword—the two-handed kind she'd heard Highlanders preferred—lurking in the pitch darkness of the upper floors. The image alone was enough to keep her from going up there, or letting the twins anywhere near the old wing, ever again. Thank goodness it was only a story.

"Wow," Alex replied, taking a step back. "I guess not."

Lara had heard enough. "Come on, kids. This gentleman is busy."

"But Mom, he's telling us about the ghost at..." Alex blurted out. Dismay flashed across his features right before his sister elbowed him in the ribs.

"It's almost Halloween," Amy gritted out with a tight smile. "Everyone knows lots of ghost stories."

"Yes, they do," Alex agreed, recovering quickly. Including stories about Cairn Dubh, it appeared.

"Thanks for keeping them entertained," Lara told the man, who'd watched the byplay with an interested grin.

"'Twas no trouble at all, Missus," he told her.

Lara raised an eyebrow to collect the twins. As she walked them toward the farmers' stands, she admonished, "Don't believe everything you hear."

Alex and Amy looked at each other, then back to her. "We won't," Amy responded for the pair.

Lara pursed her lips, hiding a grin. The twins definitely knew more than they were telling. Yet, they didn't seem frightened, so why should she? "Okay, what's for dinner?" she added, hoping for a change of subject. With the twins' contributions mostly involving groans and scrunched up noses as they demanded, "What's that?" over every unfamiliar vegetable, she started filling her basket.

A few minutes later, Ian's voice came from behind her. "You look like you could use a hand."

She glanced around in surprise just as Alex and Amy pivoted and threw themselves at him.

He caught them deftly, hooked an arm under theirs, and whirled them around.

Lara couldn't get over how strong he must be to lift both kids at once, much less to hang on to them while they spun. His bunched arm and shoulder muscles under his fisherman's sweater would make any woman drool, but Lara couldn't stop ogling his jeans covering the bunch and flex of his ass and thigh muscles as he turned. He laughed as the kids shrieked with excitement. The sound of his voice made her heart melt and her thighs clench.

Ian brought the giggling twins in for a landing, and then reached for her basket. "Let me carry that for you."

"Oh, I couldn't," she objected, though in truth, the basket was starting to pull on her arms and shoulders. She shifted it from one elbow to the other and grasped the handle with her free hand, trying to lighten the load on her arm. "You must have your own shopping to do."

"I do, but I can pick up the few things I need as we go along." He grinned and peered past her white knuckles. "Or I can just eat with you. You've got enough in here to feed a small army."

"Or two nine-year-olds."

"Almost ten," Alex added, proudly, straightening up and lifting his chin.

Ian held out a hand, palm down, by Alex's head, as if measuring the boy's growth. "Ten? I'm impressed."

"But not for four more months," Amy added.

"That's not a very long time, now is it?" Ian asked her.

She preened under his attention, smiling and curling a lock of hair around her finger as she shook her head.

God, that started so young!

It struck Lara again how Amy responded to Ian. Alex, too. They were completely comfortable with him, and, in Alex's case at least, seemed much happier and less resentful of their father's absence, even today. Especially today.

Ian always seemed fond of the twins, but the gleam in his eye made her hope it was more than fondness. He really liked them, and not just because they shared his loss. Or was it all a show to impress their mother? Surely he was smart enough to know they were the most important thing in the world to her.

Ian led the twins off on a turnip-hunting expedition, telling them as they walked away about the Scottish origin of the Halloween jack-o'lantern.

Lara's heart twisted in her chest. Their father should have been the one filling their heads full of tall tales. But he wasn't here, and hadn't been for a year. And Ian seemed determined to be a very acceptable substitute, at least for the kids.

For her, as well? *I'm here, too.* His words echoed in her mind. She had mourned long enough. She couldn't let Angus's memory keep her from a happy future. She had no doubt he would want her to live a full life, including falling in love and marrying again. Despite his reason for marrying her, he'd taken his vows seriously and they'd grown close over time. She would never stop loving the father of her children, but she hoped someone else would eventually fill her heart as he once had.

Was that someone Ian?

~

"Mom, can we get a dog?" Alex's question, in his most plaintive voice, preceded him as he bounded into the kitchen, where Lara was making dinner.

Lara glanced up from cutting potatoes into cubes to

roast along with the chicken already in the oven. "A dog? What kind of dog?"

Alex shrugged. "Oh, I don't know. A big one."

Lara froze. "A big one? Why do you want a big one?" A big one like the ghost hound she feared they'd been following around?

"I dunno. But we live in Scotland, so we should have a big Scottish dog, shouldn't we?"

She set the knife aside and concentrated on her son. "And where have you seen a big Scottish dog to make you want one?"

"Um, I dunno. Around." Alex shifted his weight from one foot to the other.

Sure, around. "Where around?" In the old wing, perhaps?

"Just around. Maybe one of the kids at school has one."

She crossed her arms. "Maybe? You're not sure?"

"No." He went from giving her his best wide-eyed "poor me, I have no puppy" face to studying the floor.

"We have a cat." And maybe a mouse. "We don't need a dog."

Alex straightened. "We do!"

Lara leaned a hip against the counter. "Why not a little dog?" This ought to be good.

"Because…a big dog would be better. And it would protect us, right?"

Did Alex think they needed protection? "And who would take care of this big Scottish dog if we got one?"

"We would. Amy and me." Alex hooked a thumb over his shoulder, indicating, no doubt, his absent sister.

"Amy and I," she corrected him.

"Amy and I. *Pul-eeze*, mom?"

Lara slid the potatoes into the pan and reached for a garlic bulb to keep from meeting his pleading gaze. He knew very well how effective it was. "Like you take care of your room? And your sister's is even worse. I don't think so." She freed a few cloves and smashed them with the flat of the knife to remove the skin, then started mincing. Their scent filled the air. Garlic was supposed to keep vampires away. Did it work on ghosts?

"We'll do better. We promise."

She paused and gave her son a direct look. "Do you think Amy wants you making promises for her without her knowledge and consent?"

"What's consent?"

Just when she thought Alex was turning into a genius diabolical man-child, he turned back into a nine-year-old boy again. "Agreement."

"She agrees."

"Oh? How do you know that?" She mixed the minced garlic with the potatoes, some olive oil and salt, then slid the pan into the oven.

"We talked about this right after…anyway, she knew you'd ask who'd take care of it and want us to keep our rooms clean, too."

After what? She let that slide. "If you both knew I'd ask, why aren't you doing it already? You could have already convinced me you could handle the responsibility. Now you have to do better for a while and wait for me to notice."

Alex's face fell. "Really? We can't get a dog and then keep our rooms cleaner?"

Lara shook her head, biting back a smile. "Nope. You have to prove to me you can handle the responsibility. Then I'll think about it."

"But…"

"Dinner's in an hour. Is your homework finished?"

"Not yet," Alex muttered, looking down again.

"Then I suggest you get busy."

Alex hurried away. Lara watched him go, torn between the urge to laugh at how cute he'd been and worry about where the idea had come from for a big dog. He'd just confirmed her suspicion that he and his sister had seen Fergus. Whether they'd seen the painting upstairs, as she suspected, or, as Alex had clearly hoped she'd believe, just a friend's dog—which was also possible, she supposed—the twins had apparently decided no Scottish estate was complete without its resident deerhound, and Alex had been elected to broach the subject with her.

Lara washed the oil and garlic off her hands, then pulled a stool out from under the granite island's bar and settled on to it to think. No doubt, if they stayed here once the renovation was done, the subject would come up again. But the idea of getting a dog—any dog, any sized dog— meant commitment. Permanence. Putting down real roots. A dog—a real one, not a ghost—in the house implied this was home and always would be.

She wasn't ready for that kind of no-going-back decision. Since the notion had occurred to her, she'd sort of given herself until the renovation was finished to be totally, utterly certain she and the twins would stay in Scotland. As much as she missed her family and California, she was still fascinated with Scotland, its customs and its people. The twins were doing well in a good school. That was very important to her.

And she was getting more and more fascinated with a certain Scotsman. She'd best be careful. Getting involved with him could result in a longer commitment than she'd ever have to make to a dog.

CHAPTER 9

On Monday, Rollo and his crew arrived early to work on the south wall's footings. By the time Lara returned from taking the kids to school, shouting and banging and motor noises filled the air.

Caitlin showed up a few minutes later. "I hope they're not going to keep that up all day," she complained as she dropped a bag of scones on Lara's kitchen table.

Lara poured tea and shook her head. "We won't get much done if they do."

She and Caitlin intended to finish the rough cataloging today. They still had to photograph about half of the artifacts on the top floor. Lara would do most of that, while Caitlin made notes describing the details of each item.

Lara suspected, based on Caitlin's expression as she examined each item and some comments mumbled to herself, Caitlin already knew enough about the contents of those rooms to piece together the story of why they were there. Which should give her some idea why they had been walled up in the first place. But so far, Caitlin wasn't talking, even to answer Lara's direct questions. Caitlin kept putting her off by saying she needed to consult with this person or that. Her hesitation might be a legitimate—maybe she wasn't certain about what they were finding. Or it could be a well-intentioned ploy to keep Lara from getting her hopes up. Either way, if she'd shared any speculations with Ian, well, he wasn't talking either.

Ian. Lara sighed and let her attention wander to a much more pleasant topic. He was wonderful at the market Saturday. Not only had he carried her shopping basket, he kept the twins entertained and out of trouble. Once Ian joined them, they'd stuck close to him, and she'd been spared their buy-me-this duet.

Best of all had been the looks Ian gave her over their heads. Though he kept the conversation light, there was something in his eyes. A hunger she hadn't seen since the early years of her marriage to Angus. Those looks were exciting, and a little frightening, promising that later, when they were alone, Ian had things to say…and do…just to her. She couldn't wait.

Too bad Alex came down with a tummy ache, or dinner and the rest of her evening might have been much more fun. Instead of spending at least part of the night in Ian's arms, she'd spent most of it cleaning up after and comforting her violently sick son. He'd finally emptied out and fallen asleep about three. But between concern for Alex, memories of Ian's heated glances, and regret for the missed opportunity to find out if she was reading him right, Lara tossed and turned the rest of the night. Thankfully, the next morning, Alex seemed completely over whatever it was that kept him up half the night. After crackers and tea, he'd demanded juice and a scone, then more water. By then he'd been fine. Amy never came down with Alex's affliction, thank goodness!

That afternoon, Lara had taken a nap and dreamed of Ian. He'd been a very naughty man. She'd awakened sweating and achingly empty where, in her dream, Ian had touched and licked and suckled, driving her mad until he'd taken her with one powerful thrust that left her gasping. Lara could only hope the reality, if it ever happened, would be half as good as she'd dreamed. In his last years, her sex life with Angus had become routine—satisfying, but a bit, frankly, boring. She almost giggled when "thinking of England" popped into her head. Fantasizing about Ian reminded her how good it could be to take a man to her bed. She had a feeling Ian would never allow staring at the ceiling.

Her core clenched, and she dragged her attention back to Caitlin, who still complained about the racket Rollo's crew was making.

"They'll scare old Fergus right out of wherever he's hiding," Caitlin declared.

Lara's jaw dropped. "Fergus? Do you think the ghost is Fergus? A hound? Is that possible?" She shook her head. "What am I saying? I'm talking like the ghost is real."

Caitlin laughed. "Maybe it is. And if it is, maybe Fergus in the painting became Fergus, the ghost. I think old Fergus can go wherever he likes. You said you thought the twins saw him and chased him back into the old wing after Ian broke in there. You'll see him in here, sooner or later."

"I'd rather see him in the old wing—or not at all."

"Ach, the ghost is not supposed to be a bad sort."

"Really? You should have heard the tale the ironmonger told Alex at the market. The ghost is the laird's most loyal warrior, and he's got a broadsword twice as big as Alex and a battle cry that'll freeze yer blood. Ugh. Now that I recall his story, I'm not sure we should go back in there."

"The tale he told you is crap," Caitlin snorted, rolling the 'r' and giving the word an extra dollop of disgust. "According to the legend, the ghost won't do anything at all, unless the laird wills it. Likely he's just curious, having been closed up over there for so long."

"And after all these years, who is the laird he'd obey?"

Caitlin drummed her fingers on the tabletop and stared off into space. In a moment, she stopped, glanced at Lara and told her, "Why, you, I imagine, since you own this place now."

"So if I will the ghost to go away? To move on to wherever ghosts go when they finish haunting—or whatever they're supposed to do while still in this dimension...?"

"I dinna ken. That might be the one thing not possible," she added, her tone shifting from spinning tall tales to matter-of-fact. "After all, we really don't know who or what it is or why it's still here, do we?"

"I can't believe I'm sitting here having a serious conversation about a ghost. Maybe even a ghost dog, for crying out loud."

"Not just a dog. A hound, he is," Caitlin corrected, "and a fierce and proud one at that, judging by the painting we found. Much loved and respected, I'd wager. Maybe that's why it's a friendly ghost."

Lara grunted. "Is there such a thing?"

Caitlin smiled. "You're in Scotland, lass. Many things are possible here that are believed to be impossible anywhere else."

Lara flinched from a sudden vision of the stag staring at the old wing before bolting into the woods. Deerhounds were bred to chase and bring down deer. In hindsight, as weird as it seemed, Lara couldn't help but think somehow that stag had been aware of Fergus's presence. "Do you think the ghost…Fergus…will do anything on Halloween?" She shuddered.

"I can't say." Caitlin shrugged and finished her tea. "But as laird, I expect you can." She stood. "Come on, let's try to get some work done."

A loud thump, followed by Rollo swearing, got them moving.

Lara stood and picked up her camera. "Maybe it'll be quieter up there."

~

Ian arrived at Cairn Dubh in time to see the bucket of a bobcat, which was supposed to be trenching around the outside of the old wing, overextend and bang into the wall. Ian jumped out of his car and jogged over, waving his arms to catch the operator's attention.

"What in hell do you think you're doing?"

The machine made so much racket, Ian was certain the man could not hear a word he said, but he must've read his lips. He gave a two fingered salute and backed the bobcat away from the wall. Rollo appeared from around the corner and rapped on the driver's door. The driver cut the motor.

"Easy there, lad," Rollo said, his voice loud in the sudden silence. "We're trying to preserve the grand old thing, not knock it down."

"Sorry, mate," the man answered. "The track rolled over a buried rock and shifted the whole damn 'cat."

Ian narrowed his eyes at Rollo, who told the man, "Sorry doesn't cut it. Pay attention to what you're doing."

The man nodded, restarted the engine, and went back to work.

Ian and Rollo watched him start to clear some ground outside of the existing trench to expose whatever had caught the 'cat's track, then Rollo beckoned for Ian to follow him.

Once they got away from the source of the noise, Rollo pointed out the scar the bobcat had left on the outside of the north wall. "Opposite here is where we found those loose slate tiles. Anything look amiss on the outside to you?"

"Now that you mention it, it looks like the wall has been repaired right about there."

"Maybe we should do a little digging on the other side of this wall."

"Agree. The floor was disturbed for a reason."

They both grabbed shovels and a pry bar out of the pile of well-used tools in Rollo's lorry. Inside the structure, the thick stone walls muted, somewhat, the roar of the bobcat outside. He recognized Lara and Caitlin's voices bouncing down the stairs. Their echo distorted them enough, he could not understand what they were saying, but hearing Lara's voice warmed him.

Rollo led him to the spot where the slate floor tiles lay askew. "Let's lift these away," he said and propped his shovel against the nearby wall.

Ian did the same and bent to work the pry bar under the edge of the stone. With some effort, it lifted. "It's a bloody good thing these aren't any larger, or we'd need equipment in here to move them," he huffed as Rollo got the other side up and they propped the stone against the wall, out of their way.

"I'd say we need to remove these three," Rollo pointed out, "and we'll have enough room to trench along the outer wall."

"Let's do it, then."

They moved the second stone and started on the third when the lasses came down the stairs.

"We thought we heard voices down here," Caitlin said.

"You found us," Ian replied, his gaze on Lara. She smiled, then frowned at the exposed dirt behind him.

"What are you doing?"

Ian assumed the answer was obvious. "We're going to see what's under here."

"Oooh," Caitlin cooed, "What if it's treasure?" Then she laughed.

Ian agreed with the laugh. They had enough treasure upstairs.

"Most likely a trash midden, if ye ask me," Rollo interjected.

Rollo had seen all of the hidden rooms' contents— he'd strung the lights in them and on the rest of the top two floors —but Ian was not concerned he'd gossip about what he'd seen, or about anything they found. And with a treasure hidden upstairs, Ian doubted they'd find another one buried here.

"Well?" Caitlin tapped her foot. "Get on with it."

Ian grabbed a shovel and offered it to her. "Why don't you start?"

While Lara snickered, Caitlin wiped her hands as if brushing off dirt. "Nay, laddie. Digging is man's work."

Ian grinned at Lara, then pushed the shovel toward his cousin again. "Are ye sure? There might be gold and diamonds."

"Or medieval indoor plumbing. No thank ye. Besides, Lara and I still have aplenty to do upstairs. We just came down to see what you were up to. But give us a shout if ye find anything interesting."

Ian stabbed the point of the shovel in the dirt. "Aye, we'll be sure to do that, we will."

Caitlin tossed her head and waved for Lara to follow, then headed back upstairs.

"You can stay if you like," Ian told her. Most lasses liked to watch a man work, after all. If it helped Lara act on her attraction to him, he'd dig all the way to China.

"I'd better go help your cousin," she demurred. "But I can't wait to see what you find."

"If anything…"

"Yes, well. I'll see you later. Rollo." Lara nodded to his companion and turned away.

Rollo nodded and started to loosen the dirt around the edges.

Once Lara was far enough up the stairs he could no longer see her, Ian dug in beside him.

Rollo glanced at the stairs, then back at Ian, cocked a speculative eyebrow and grinned.

"Knock it off," Ian warned him.

They worked side by side in silence, careful in case they did encounter anything of interest, removing the soil layer by layer. Two feet down, Rollo crouched and smoothed away dirt and crumbled mortar a few inches from the front facade of the wall. Then he stilled and rocked back on his heels. "Ach, bollocks. Take a look and tell me what you see here."

Ian crouched beside him and brushed at the dirt, exposing more of what had caught Rollo's eye. "Christ, is that what I think it is?"

"Aye, I'm wondering the same, lad. And if it's human, we've got a problem."

"Surely they didn't bury some poor unfortunate soul in here."

"We won't ken until we move more of this dirt."

Ian huffed out a breath. "Let's clear a bit more over this way. If it's an animal, maybe we'll find a skull pretty quickly."

As they worked, Ian found squared-off border stones running vertically and realized the skeleton had been placed in a walled-up portal that must have once been a ground floor doorway to the outside. He pointed them out to Rollo. "What do you want to bet the rock the bobcat got caught on was a threshold stone just outside of here."

"I won't take that bet. I think you're right. We can check outside later."

They dug some more, moving away from the wall about a foot, and found a long leg bone. "We need to lift the next slate," Ian said, pointing. "The body seems to lie in that direction, toward the wall."

They moved the slate. Now they knew what they were digging for, they made quick work of excavating and carefully exposed the profile of the rest of the skeleton.

"Holy Mary," Rollo muttered. "Someone buried an animal in this room. That's better than a person, I guess."

The girls came down the stairs chatting about lunch, and Ian called them over.

"What do ye make of this?"

"That looks like a coyote or wolf's skull," Lara announced, bending over to study the visible bone. "We studied them in a zoology class I took in college."

Caitlin crouched in front of her and pointed a finger at the midline of the skeleton. "And look at how carefully it's stretched out and positioned. That's meticulous work."

"This animal was important to someone," Ian mused.

Caitlin frowned at the bones for a moment, then her eyebrows lifted and her mouth dropped open as she jumped to her feet. "Nay!" she shrieked and clamped a hand over her mouth. "I ken what it is," she added through her fingers, then pointed at the bones again. "Look at the size. Imagine it filled out with muscle and hair. It's a deerhound. It's Fergus!"

Ian frowned. "Why would they bury the laird's favorite hound right inside a walled-up doorway?"

Rollo stuck his hands in his pockets. "Likely to guard the place. They might have thought if his body blocked the doorway, his ghost would protect what's hidden behind those walls," he added, indicating the secret staircase and rooms with a lift of his chin.

Lara covered her face with both hands for a moment. "Surely they didn't kill him for this."

"Probably not," Ian said quietly, hoping that was true.

"He was left here to protect the place and the things these people held dear," Rollo added. "Likely he died of old age at a convenient time, so they put him to work in the afterlife."

Lara cocked her head to the side, studying the grave. "Look at the way he's facing…toward the hidden rooms."

"I can't believe I'm about to ask this question, but if he's supposed to be guarding things, why haven't we had any problems up there?" Ian glanced toward the public stairs they'd all used many times to ascend to the first floor.

Lara regarded Ian. "Didn't you tell me the legend says the ghost obeys the laird?" She turned to Caitlin. "You did, too. And every time we've been up there, you've been with me."

Caitlin cut a glance toward Ian, then glanced down, earning a frown from him. What else had she told Lara?

"You weren't around when I put in the lights," Rollo objected with a frown.

"But Lara wanted them there, right?" Caitlin's eye's sparked defiance as she looked from Rollo to Ian, then at the bones.

"This is all just silly," Lara objected. "For one thing," she said, ticking off points on her fingers, "whoever heard of a ghost dog…hound," she corrected with a sideways glance at Caitlin. "And two, how would a ghost…hound…know enough to obey the laird and three, how would he know who was laird, and…oh, this is nuts." She threw up her hands. "We should either move those bones outside and give them a proper burial or cover them back up where they are. Since someone clearly wanted him in there like that, let the poor hound rest in peace."

Rollo grabbed his shovel. "The hound has done no damage to anything around him, so I say we leave him be where he is."

"Someone did a lot of work to place him there," Caitlin observed. "Whether he's guarding Cairn Dubh's secrets or not, we shouldn't disturb his bones. Or not any more than we already have."

"If this is Fergus and he is the ghost," Rollo added, "he won't like being moved. Certainly no' right before Halloween." He plunged the shovel's blade into the mound of dirt he and Ian had created along the base of the leaning slate flooring stones they'd carefully removed.

Ian studied the skull's profile, then the ribs, pelvic and leg bones whose curved surfaces protruded slightly from the supporting gravel and dirt like twigs in a mosaic of pebbles. "We should at least get some photographs of this."

"I'll go back up and get my camera," Caitlin offered and left at a run.

Ian looked at Lara. "It's your decision."

"Leave him be," Lara said and nodded. "And do not tell the twins he's here."

~

Back at his office that afternoon, Ian tried to focus on another project, but his thoughts kept returning to Lara, the hound's bones they'd found, and Fergus's ghost. Up to now, it had all seemed like a touching tale, but seeing those bones made it all too real. What would happen on Halloween, when spirits were reputed to walk the earth? Were Lara and the twins in any danger?

Not if he believed the tales saying the ghost obeyed the laird.

Lara was laird of the keep now. As long as Fergus accepted that, she and the twins would be fine. And if he didn't? Ian ran a hand through his hair. Old folk tales and the upcoming holiday were putting ridiculous notions in everyone's mind. Here he sat, thinking seriously about the threat posed by a ghost that probably didn't exist. A ghost hound, of all the crazy ideas. But Lara said the twins had been acting strangely since he'd started work in the old wing. And then, on the stairs, he and Lara had felt that odd draft…and again in the hidden room after they'd decided to leave Fergus's painting where they found it…nay, there had been too much talk about a ghost, about Halloween. Besides, what could one ghost hound do?

Ian could think of only one way to put all this nonsense to rest. He would find a way to be out at Cairn Dubh Halloween night.

He shifted the floor plan on the drafting table before him. He had expected to finish the detailed drawing today, but his heart wasn't in it. He glanced at the piles of paperwork stacked on his desk. He needed to hire a partner, and soon, but all he could think about was Cairn Dubh…and Lara—Lara taking off her ring at Blane and Cassie's wedding, her fingertips brushing his palm, her in his arms on the stairs, her lips a breath away from his—and so much more that he hoped for.

With a growl, he left the office in search of coffee. His secretary, Lenore, would bring him some if he asked, but he needed to stretch his legs and get his mind off of Lara. This time of the afternoon, the few people about would be headed home from work or to the market, or just enjoying the late-day sun peeking out between some clouds. Ian didn't have the sidewalk to himself, but he didn't mind.

Until he saw Cassie's mother headed his way, frowning as soon as she noticed him. He continued on, knowing the confrontation was inevitable at this point, and pasted on his friendliest smile.

"Good afternoon, Mrs. Crawley," he greeted her.

"Is it? After you conspired with my daughter and son-in-law to elope? To leave their families out of the ceremony? How could you? A mother dreams of seeing her daughter married, and thanks to you, I missed it."

"How could I refuse a friend?" Ian responded, knowing if she was already playing the guilt card, the rest of this conversation was not going to go well.

"You could have talked them into a delay. I had such grand plans."

"I did suggest waiting, but they were insistent." And he didn't agree with any of the grand plans, but Ian knew better than to mention that.

"Hmmph. And I hear you brought that young widow with you. For shame."

So if she couldn't get a reaction from him about the elopement, she'd come at him through Lara? Ian took a breath. "I did, and there was no shame involved, ma'am. The happy couple asked for her."

"Indeed? It seems to me all too easy for you to take advantage of her, what with her husband having just passed…"

"A year ago," Ian ground out, his temper starting to rise despite his good intentions.

"Keep in mind, Ian Paterson, this is a small village. If you overstep, we'll ken."

"I wouldn't dream of it," Ian responded through clenched teeth. "Now, if you'll excuse me, I've business to attend to."

"Aye," she said, and sniffed, "I imagine you do." Ian stepped around her and went on his way, seething. If this was the reaction his interest in Lara got from the people in the village who'd known him since he was in nappies, he didn't want to think about how Lara would react if she found out about him from anyone else.

He could imagine a future with her, but not if he didn't carefully handle telling her.

He'd tell her tomorrow, he decided. Since his uncle died and he had no male cousins, he was the last male of his line. She needed to ken who he was. What his grandfather had insisted he was supposed to be. His family's connection to her estate. All of it. He couldn't stand the suspense any longer. He had to know if she could accept his heritage, and Halloween, the night for telling old tales, would be the perfect time to lay it all out.

She planned to take the twins into the village to trick-or-treat. He'd come over once they'd returned home, and they'd talk after the kids went to bed, zoned out on sugar. Surely, they'd sleep soundly after indulging in Halloween candy. And he'd be there if Fergus decided to show himself to the adults. As long as Lara didn't kick him out before the hound had a chance to appear. If he didn't accept Lara as laird, maybe Ian would do.

CHAPTER 10

*L*ara laughed as the twins presented themselves in their ragged old clothes for her inspection. Scottish children dressed in tattered clothes and ghoulish makeup as their Halloween costumes to go ''guising', so the twins had insisted on following the custom. No superheroes or witches and warlocks for them this year. They'd even found suitable turnips at the farmers' market—with Ian's help—before Alex had gotten sick and her wish for an evening with Ian had gone by the wayside. She'd drawn the line at allowing the twins to walk around with actual candles in their neep lanterns. She'd inserted battery-powered tea lights, justifying her choice by telling them they wouldn't be blown out by a ghost's breath or the spooky Halloween wind. Amy looked skeptical, but Alex just shrugged.

"You've memorized your rhyme, right? You can't just yell 'trick or treat' to get candy. People here expect more from their visiting ghouls."

"We've got it, Mom," Amy informed her with an eye roll at her brother. "Dad told us about it last year before he... left for California."

Lara's heart clenched. Okay, message received. She ruffled Amy's hair, then Alex's, a silent show of sympathy and shared pain. Trick-or-treating had been out of the question last year. They'd returned to California, to family, and to the funeral. Her mother had offered to take the twins around the neighborhood, but no one had been in the mood for ghosts and goblins. She figured they were making progress if it sounded like fun this year.

"Let's go then," she told them and grabbed her keys. Tonight, she'd leave the house dark and locked up, making it clear to anyone who ventured this far out of town that no one was home to hand out goodies, at least not while she and the twins were out and about. If Angus were still alive, he could have taken door duty, or escorted the twins. But he was gone, and Lara had to make this work on her own.

In the village, a party had been set up in the main square with food, drink, and games. But first, the kids would make the rounds of the nearby homes and businesses to collect enough candy to keep them on a sugar high for days. Then the adults would keep an eye on the miniature ghouls while they ran around the square, playing games and chasing each other, until time to go home.

Over an hour later, Lara encountered Becky as they returned to the square from dropping the twins' bags of plunder in the car.

"Are they wound up on sugar, yet?" Becky asked as the twins raced toward some school friends.

How they recognized anyone was beyond Lara. All the kids looked much the same in their old clothes and dirty faces. A few had on slouchy hats, as well.

"Getting there," Lara assured her. "Are yours here?"

"Ach, nay. They're too old and sophisticated for such as this. But I still enjoy watching the bairns have a grand time, so here I am."

"I'm glad. We can keep each other company."

"And keep an eye on...how did you describe them? Trouble and Double-trouble?"

"Indeed."

"Speaking of trouble, Ian's here, ye ken."

Lara swallowed, trying to keep her interest from being obvious. "He is?" Then her stomach sank as she recalled how little she knew about him. "I didn't think he had children."

"He doesn't. He's never married. But he sponsors the 'dunking-for-apples' tub every year. It is one of the most entertaining events on the square...though we haven't managed to drown any lads or lasses...yet."

Lara summoned the energy to laugh, despite still feeling a twinge in her chest after jumping to the conclusion that Ian taking part in the Halloween festivities meant he came with a wife and children of his own—none of which he'd mentioned. She had given herself a fright. Becky just confirmed he wasn't married, she told herself, recalling the very unmarried and available vibes he'd been sending her. Not that men didn't lie about their marital status every day, but she felt certain Ian would not. Too many people knew him too well around here. And, well, Ian just wouldn't. He also didn't have kids, though she would not have minded, as long as he'd mentioned them sometime in the months since she'd met him. She breathed a sigh of relief, then laid a hand over her heart.

He was here.

She hadn't known he would be part of the celebration. Other than a passing thought about what the ghost of Fergus might do on Halloween, and wishing Ian would be there to…well, actually, she didn't know what she expected him to be able to do about a ghost. If there was a ghost. And she'd been too busy all day to even consider where Ian might spend the holiday.

Lara saw the knowing grin spread across Becky's ruddy face and realized her own must have reflected the thoughts flitting through her mind, and her desire for Ian.

"Did ye think he'd spend the evening at home? With all this going on? Or," Becky added with a sly smile, "show up at your door, looking for a treat?"

Lara cut her a glance and rolled her eyes. "Seriously? Don't be ridiculous. Besides, the house is locked up. He couldn't get in if he wanted to." Not that he would. He hadn't mentioned coming back to the house tonight, even after all the talk about Fergus when they found the hound's bones. She was on her own until Halloween ended. "Are ghosts allowed to walk all night until sunup, or at 12:01, once it is no longer All Hallows Eve, do they go back to wherever they came from?" If so, she was tempted to keep the twins out past midnight.

Becky burst out laughing. "Ye are not serious. Are ye?"

No. Yes. "Of course not."

"I'm happy to see you embracing Scottish customs, but dinnae go overboard, aye?"

Did Becky, like Ian, speak with a thicker accent when she got nervous? What did she have to be nervous about? They were just talking about ghosts…on Halloween.

"Oh, for heaven's sake," Lara muttered, more to herself than Becky. "This conversation has gotten way out of hand."

"Aye," Becky said, taking her arm and urging her forward. "Let's go back to talking about something more fun, like Ian Paterson."

She could see where Becky was leading her. The twins had gravitated toward the one adult in the crowd they knew well and idolized, and were currently hanging on to Ian, watching as others bobbed for apples. It wouldn't be long before they joined in.

"Convenient, isn't it? We can watch the twins and Ian, too," Becky teased.

"I see what you're doing," Lara warned her.

"Me? I'm just walking around, doing what we said, making sure the twins stay out of trouble."

"Sure you are."

At that moment, Ian looked up from the twins and caught sight of her and Becky. A wide grin lit his face. Lara could only smile back. Becky tugged her even faster in his direction.

"Care to try?" he asked as they got close enough to hear him over children's shrieks and laughter.

"What can I win?"

Ian lifted an eyebrow, his gaze suddenly molten. But his smile and his words were more for public consumption. "An apple?"

Lara forced a laugh around the heart suddenly lodged in her throat. "I think I'll pass. But Becky, you should try it. Soaking your head might do you some good."

Becky burst out laughing again, then gave Lara a look that promised payback. "I think that's my cue to be on my way. Ian, she's all yours."

"Promise?" Ian responded, grinning at Becky, then leveling his gaze on Lara.

Lara gasped. Heat flushed her chest and traveled up her neck. Did he really just say that? In public? And did he mean it?

Becky chuckled, shook her head and wandered away.

Ian turned his gaze on Lara. "I'm only here another forty minutes, then I'm free to go. Why don't I come out to Cairn Dubh after I'm done?" He glanced down at the twins, but they were laughing, their attention on a lad who had just about gotten his teeth into an apple, then lost it and dunked his head completely into the tub trying to recapture it. "It's the perfect night to go ghost hunting again," Ian said softly.

Lara gave a nervous chuckle and glanced at the twins to make sure they hadn't overheard, since they'd demand to be included if they thought that was why Ian had come over. Then she glanced back at Ian and noted his grin. Did he really mean ghost hunting? The image of Fergus's bones flashed before her eyes. Oh no, not a chance. But she would feel safer with Ian there, at least until midnight...or dawn. Why not, indeed? She could get the twins home, cleaned up and headed for bed by the time he arrived.

"I'll make tea."

"Ach, I've a mind for something stronger than tea."

"Whisky it will be, then." She waved to her offspring. "Time to go, kids."

"Aw, Mom," Amy complained, right on cue.

"Don't 'aww, Mom' me. You've had your fun. By the time we get home and you get cleaned up, it's going to be past your bedtime." She included Alex in the look she gave Amy. "Both of you still have school tomorrow, remember?"

Alex perked up suddenly. "Maybe when we get home, the ghost will be out and we can find out where he sleeps. Let's go!"

She traded a glance with Ian. "I sincerely hope not. See you later, Ian."

He nodded and smiled, but as she turned away, she noticed his expression morphed into a frown. She and Ian knew where the bones of a giant deerhound lay. Did he think Alex was right?

~

As she drove through the woods to the dark estate, Lara realized she should have left a light on. Not wanting to entice trick-or-treaters to an empty house was one thing. Coming home to the Addams Family mansion on Halloween was quite another. Not that Cairn Dubh looked anything like the haunted house on TV. But still.

Nights were so much darker here than in California—especially this time of year. Especially on this night. Oh, stop it, she told herself. You'll be jumping at shadows next.

She didn't bother putting the car in the carriage house. The wind had picked up, but the dry cold air did not presage snow. Besides, she wasn't sure she could face the dark confines of that building. It took all her nerve to put on a cheerful demeanor as she and the twins walked toward the shadowed front entrance.

Even Alex fell quiet as they approached it. "Spooky, huh?" she teased, hoping for a laugh. Both kids just nodded. In unison.

Like that wasn't spooky enough.

"Okay," she called, unlocking the door, "we're home. Let's do this!" She stepped in and flipped on the foyer lights. Everything looked perfectly normal. No large deerhound's ghost barred their way.

"Remember what I said," she told the kids as she went forward, flipping on the hall light, the light above the stairs, and every other light switch she could easily reach. "Clean up first, then bed." When they didn't answer, she glanced around.

Alex had closed the front door and stood with his back to it, Amy at his side. Was it her imagination, or did they look…not scared…surprised? Nervous?

"Come on," she urged and pointed to the stairs. "Go."

"Um, maybe you should come with us," Amy suggested.

Lara paused and studied the pair. Really, Halloween or no, this had to stop. "Let's take your candy to the kitchen and make some cocoa first, how about that?"

They nodded and followed her silently. Weird. Once in the kitchen, bright overhead and under-cabinet lights blazing, they seemed to relax. She poured their candy out on the table, warning them, "No more than three pieces each for now. Divide it up however you like."

She went about making the hot cocoa, thinking about how Angus used to enjoy teasing the twins as they negotiated—okay, fought—for their favorite candy. In the end, all three would wind up with a pile in front of them and be in a sugar coma within thirty minutes. She was counting on that happening tonight.

She'd like them to be upstairs and settled before Ian arrived, not begging to go with him into the old wing to look for Fergus's ghost. Although...the way they'd acted when they arrived home made her wonder if they'd seen him already. And if they had, why hadn't she? Would Fergus ever show himself to anyone past puberty?

By the time she set a steaming mug beside each child, they had created two fairly sizable piles in front of them, and a smaller one off to the side.

"Those are for you," Alex explained.

Lara swallowed the lump in her throat and ruffled their hair. "Thank you, kids." Despite what they said, she knew the twins had created that pile to remember a happy time with their father.

She sat with them and sipped her cocoa, enjoying its sweet warmth after the chill of the village square. The twins kept trading looks and watching her out of the corner of their eyes. Finally, she'd had enough.

"He's here, isn't he?"

"Who?" Amy asked, all innocence.

"There's no one here," Alex added right after.

"Fergus. Something is spooking you two. I'm going to assume a ghostly deerhound is sitting where you can see him. Do you think he'd like some cocoa, too?" Lara wanted to congratulate herself for keeping her cool, but then both sets of the twins' eyes swiveled toward the same spot at the entrance to the hallway leading to the old wing. A chill ran down Lara's spine.

"Chocolate is bad for dogs," Alex reminded her. "Besides, I don't think ghosts drink cocoa," Amy whispered.

Neither twin reacted when she named and described the ghost. Seriously? So they knew about Fergus already? They'd be impossible if they knew about the skeleton in the floor. Lara finished her cocoa. "Okay, I get it," she said and chuckled. "You two are playing with me. If you're done with your drinks, it's time to get cleaned up."

She took the kids upstairs, all the while wondering if she would feel a cold breeze across the back of her neck, or wiry hair brushing the back of her hand. Ridiculous.

Amy took her shower after Alex, while Lara tucked Alex in. He always wanted to go first, complaining his sister took forever. Out of curiosity, Lara had once timed their showers for a week. They'd used exactly the same amount of time…and water.

Over the sound of the shower spray next door, Lara thought she heard the front door. Ian had made good time.

She went to the top of the stairs and called down, "Make yourself at home. I'll be down in a few minutes." She headed back toward the twins' bedrooms and didn't hear an answer. But she didn't think much of it, since Amy chose that moment to exit the bathroom in a cloud of steam and a terrycloth robe.

"It's too steamy in there to blow my hair dry," she complained. "It'll take forever."

"Use the dryer in my bathroom," Lara told her. "Then go to bed. Lights out."

In moments, the whine of her blow dryer filled the upstairs hallway. Lara headed down the stairs, eager to escape the noise. And to find Ian's arms. She hated to admit it, but the twins' playacting, and please God, let them have been playacting, had spooked her. She needed a hug. Ian's hug. His kiss. She no longer wore her ring. Maybe it was time she admitted to herself she was ready for a whole lot more, like what the heat in his gaze had promised earlier tonight. She'd been kidding herself about keeping him off limits. If Ian was here with her tonight, they were definitely on.

Where was he? She expected him to be in the library, but the room was dark and cold, no fire laid. The kitchen, still brightly lit and redolent with the rich scent of cocoa, was empty, too. Three piles of candy lay where the twins left them.

She went down the hall to the entrance to the old wing's ground floor. It was dark in there, too. "Ian?"

When he didn't answer, she shrugged and headed back to the library. She must've imagined hearing the door. She laid the fire and lit it. In moments, flickering flames bounced light and shadows on the walls and bookshelves around her and her nose picked up the scent of peat.

Someone knocked on the front door. Finally. Lara replaced the fireplace screen, hurried to the door and opened it.

Ian stood there.

Lara instantly got lost in the smile on his lips and in relief. He was here. She would not have to get through the rest of this night alone.

With snow drifting down behind him, Ian gave her a moment, then murmured, "Are you going to ask me in?"

"Oh, of course. It's just…I thought…"

"Mo-o-om," Amy called, her voice echoing down the stairs. "I'm done."

"Good night, Amy," she answered without taking her gaze from Ian's, motioned him inside, and closed the door behind him.

Ian glanced up the stairs. "The coast is clear," he said softly, "and there's somethin' I've been dying to do since I saw you at the fair." He took her hand, one eyebrow cocked as if waiting for her permission.

He was going to kiss her. His words and his touch sent tingles sizzling up her arm and across her chest. She softened her stance and leaned toward him. "Oh?"

In answer, he pulled her against his hard length and wrapped his other arm around her, then kissed her, his lips stroking over hers like velvet, her awareness spiraling down until nothing existed but Ian's mouth, the hint of apples on his breath and the rumble of a heated moan in his chest vibrating against the sudden peaks of her nipples.

When her lips parted under his, his tongue tracing her lower lip recalled her to where they were, in full view of the upstairs foyer if one of the twins came out of their room. "Not here," she squeaked and pulled out of his grasp. She led him into the library, pulling the pocket door not quite closed so she could hear if one of the twins called out. "Besides, the whisky's in here."

She poured their drinks and settled in one corner of the couch, trying for the distance she hoped would slow her heart rate back to normal. If just for a minute, she needed to think. Heated glances and hot kisses had been missing from her life for a very long time, but how much farther did she want to go with him tonight?

Ian clinked her glass. "Sláinte," he toasted her.

"And to you," she answered. "How did the rest of the party go?"

"From where I was? Wet. And cold." He chuckled, then sipped. "That's better. Warm from the inside out." He gave a quick shudder, then grinned. "It took longer than I expected to run out of apples, though I ate as many as I could."

Lara laughed out loud. For the first time since returning home, mirth bubbled into her chest, relieving her fears.

"That's why I'm late." He reached for her hand. "I shouldn't have brought so many, or I would have been here an hour ago."

"I've been thinking about you since I got home," Lara admitted. "Wondering if you would change your mind." She hadn't changed hers. She wanted him, but with the twins upstairs, she didn't know how to do this, to entertain a man—hell, she might as well admit it—to have sex with Ian with her children upstairs. She felt awkward and needy at the same time. It had been a long year. But Ian was here, and his hand felt rough and strong and hot holding hers.

She was sure Ian had the same idea when he set his glass aside, then took hers and did the same.

She arched an eyebrow, teasing and serious all at once. "That kiss by the door was a nice start, but nowhere near enough after making me endure such a long wait." She was playing with fire, and she knew it. She expected Ian to pounce on her, but he surprised her. "Before we get too carried away, there's something I need to tell ye," he said, releasing her hand.

He suddenly looked ill at ease.

"Why? I already know you don't have a wife at home," she teased. She considered letting him talk. But she'd waited too long for the nerve to do this, and she wanted Ian's hands and mouth on her.

"It's something I've been meaning to tell ye for a while…"

"Then it can wait for a while longer, can't it?" She leaned forward. It seemed her body had decided to throw caution to the wind, even if her brain hadn't caught on to the idea quite yet. She leaned into him, wanting more. "I'm finally ready for this," she whispered and then traced a quivering finger down the side of his face and over his mouth. His lips parted enough for her to trace the inner curve of his lower lip with her fingertip while she ran her other hand down his throat and rested it on his chest. She felt his muscles flex under her palm and whispered his name. "For you, Ian…"

With an oath, he pulled her into his arms and brought his mouth down on hers.

Lara melted into his kiss. He tasted of whisky and apples and Ian. Eager to pull him closer, to feel his weight press her into the cushions, she threaded her fingers into his hair and tugged him with her as she leaned back.

While his lips teased hers, his hand traced a trail of tingles down her throat and into the vee of her sweater.

Her lips parted on a moan, letting his tongue invade her mouth and tangle with hers. Hungry for more of him, she sucked gently and he groaned, then brushed his fingertips between her breasts and covered one with his palm. She arched into his hand, willing him to tighten his grip, to stroke and tease, to touch her everywhere he could reach.

"God, lass, ye turn my brain to parritch. I need…"

"I do, too." She'd been too long without a man's hands on her skin, his scent in her nose, his taste on her tongue. Ian wanted her and she wanted him. Over the past three months, he'd shown her kindness and honesty. Now, she wanted passion.

She lost herself in the sensations as Ian explored. His fingers slipped under the hem of her sweater and stroked upward along her ribs, her bare skin heating under his touch as he whispered her name. Then he brushed her nipple and a thrill shot through to her core. When he left her mouth and kissed his way down her throat, she had no doubt where he was going, and she welcomed the brush of cool air on her overheated skin when he lifted her sweater and tugged down the lacy cup of her bra.

"Beautiful," he murmured, his gaze burning into her flesh. He lifted a molten glance to her face. "Ye slay me, lass."

He took her straining nipple in his mouth, pressing, stroking and teasing with his tongue and teeth until the urge to get both of them out of their clothes nearly overcame her. But they couldn't—she hadn't locked the door. Instead, she pulled his shirt from the waistband of his pants and shoved her hands underneath it, reveling in the flex and bunch of muscles in his back as he shifted over her to bare her other nipple and torment it as he had the first.

She raked her nails down his spine, then pressed with the heels of her hands, urging him more fully over her. She wanted…needed…the sensation of his weight on her.

He complied, covering her and holding her head in both hands as he kissed her.

She wrapped one leg over his and felt his erection press into the apex of her thighs, right where she wanted it. Ian moaned and strained against her. If not for a slightly open door and several layers of clothes, he would be inside her. The idea made her blood sing in her veins.

"God, Lara," he whispered as he rocked against her. "I've hated hiding how much I want ye. Now ye ken…"

"I want you, too, Ian," she said, and felt him still.

"But we can't, no' yet." His breathing slowed. He lifted his upper body away from her and gazed into her eyes. "First, there is something about me ye must know."

She stroked the side of his face as her heart slowed and her blood chilled. "Is it so important?"

"I think so, but you will be the judge of that. I'll feel better if ye ken before we go any farther."

Suddenly, Amy shrieked, and Alex's voice cut through the sudden silence with a yelled, "No!"

Lara and Ian jumped apart, tugging down and straightening their clothes. For one mortifying second, Lara thought the twins had walked in on them, and she with her sweater pushed up to her shoulders, but she and Ian were still alone, the door exactly as she'd left it. Thank God.

The twins didn't sound hurt, just scared, and judging by Alex's voice, outraged.

Suddenly, Fergus was standing right in front of Ian, then he bolted out the library door, not bothering to open it.

Lara swallowed her shock. "Where...?" she whispered.

"You know where," Ian barked, threw open the door and ran. Lara followed on his heels.

~

Ian's thoughts churned as he raced for the old wing. The ghost had finally appeared to fetch him and Lara. The shock of that encounter had yet to leave him, but the ghost's appearance told him what the twins were doing out of bed and roaming all the way through the house—hunting Fergus. How could they sneak by without him or their mother being aware? They could have walked in on them in the library, in the middle of what they'd finally been doing, and in the middle of the confession he'd been about to make. As he ran toward where he thought he'd heard their voices, his pulse still raced with the memory of Lara's touch, the heat of her body under his. Her scent still teased him with every breath.

Ian was fast, but so was Lara.

As they reached the wing's entry, she plowed into his back and demanded "Where?"

"Quiet," he whispered. The lights blazed, but the ground floor main hallway was empty. So were the visible rooms, including the ones near where he and Rollo had found what they presumed were Fergus's bones.

She nodded and pushed past him, the intensity of her stare as her head turned right and left telling him she expected to see some disaster had befallen the twins.

"Upstairs," Ian mouthed, crossed the hallway, his longer stride letting him get ahead of her again, and started up. He could hear Alex arguing with someone— or something— and Amy sniffling. The closer he got, the more distinctly angry Alex's voice got.

"Leave that alone!" Alex shouted.

A deeper voice, oddly muffled, answered, but Ian didn't catch what was said. No doubt, Lara could hear them, too, and her maternal instincts must be screaming for her to race up the stairs past him. Ian gave her credit for keeping her head and staying behind him. He was bigger, stronger, and better equipped to deal with any threat. The twins might have started out ghost hunting, but they'd found something decidedly human. A deep voice answered Alex, and Ian didn't think ghosts could talk. Certainly not a ghost hound.

Lara stumbled on the step below him. He twisted around to grab her arm and save her from a fall, thankful she hadn't cried out. Once she nodded she was okay, she hooked her fingers into his belt and they continued up the stairs.

When they reached the second floor, Ian could scarcely credit what he saw. Lara's quick intake of breath as she moved up next to him hinted at her shock. A man in a ski mask stood in the first open portal they'd cut into the hidden rooms, a bulging sack in one hand, likely full of treasures, his other hand empty. His stare was riveted to the giant deerhound, teeth bared, dark eyes glinting with danger, standing between him and the twins.

Alex and Amy stood off to the side of the stairs, postures stiff. Alex had stopped talking when Ian and his mother appeared, but Amy still sniffled.

Frightened, most likely. Alex seemed calm, but it was the most unnerved Ian had seen the normally confident lass behave. Her upset had the effect of making his rage at the robber burn even hotter. "What do ye think ye are doing in here?" Ian demanded.

The robber's eyes darted from Fergus to Ian and back again. "Keep that beast away from me."

Ian exchanged a look with Lara and then with each of the twins.

"Fergus has been guarding us," Alex informed them, his tone as cool as could be. "And keeping him from getting away." He indicated the burglar with a lift of his chin. "He's trying to steal our stuff."

Ian's pride in the twins grew exponentially in that moment. Imagine facing a robber armed only with attitude…and a ghost. Ian fought not to smile. This wasn't over yet. Though the robber didn't have a weapon in his hand, the twins and Lara were still in danger.

Did the robber think Fergus was real? Alive? What did he see that they did not? To Ian, Fergus looked as he always expected a ghost to look—a little transparent around the edges. Couldn't the man see that?

Ian turned back to the interloper. "Set the bag on the floor," he ordered. "Carefully. Or I'll let the hound pull ye down, and ye ken what they can do to a buck. What do ye think he'll do to ye if ye run?"

Fergus, his movement utterly, preternaturally silent, edged closer to the robber who held up both hands and the bag in defense.

Ian wondered what the robber made of that silence—if he'd noticed.

"Fergus, guard the twins." Lara choked out and moved to stand with an arm over the shoulder of each of her children, pulling them close to her and leaving Ian alone at the top of the stairs.

Fergus's head turned toward her when she moved, then his glance shifted to Ian.

The robber must've taken his brief inattention for his only opportunity. He broke for the stairway and barreled into Ian.

Ian grabbed him before he got by, swung around and

shoved him away from the stairs, then flattened him with an uppercut to the chin. The bag skittered across the floor. "Guard, Fergus," Ian ordered.

Fergus moved to it and sat, guarding it. Ian had no doubt Fergus would not let the robber pick it up again.

Ian hoped the fight would be over that fast.

But the man pushed to his knees and got one foot under him. He jumped to his feet and charged Ian, landing thudding blows to Ian's chest and shoulder, as he twisted and grappled to get to the stairs.

Ian couldn't let him get by. A fall down those hard stone steps could be deadly. He counted on Lara to keep the twins out of the way as he tangled with the robber.

The man was too close to land more than a glancing blow, but he didn't try. He pulled free and again bolted for the stairs.

Ian caught him before he took two steps, jerked him around and got in a solid punch to the head. The mask stayed in place as the man staggered back, closer to Lara and the twins.

Glancing aside, his eyes narrowed. He twisted around and grabbed Amy out of her mother's grasp.

Both the lass and her mother shrieked. Ian took an aborted step toward them as Fergus gained his feet.

The man shifted his grip on Amy to lay his forearm across her throat and backed away from Lara's reach toward the stairs. "Let me by," he demanded.

"If you hurt the lass, I will kill you," Ian warned.

"I'm going down the stairs with her," the man declared. "You will stay up here—and keep that beast with you. I'll let her go at the bottom and leave. No harm done, aye?"

"Ye will let her go now," Ian told him, "if ye want to get out of here alive."

Lara gasped and Amy whimpered. Ian ignored both.

"Fergus, the stairs," Ian ordered, hoping the robber's fear of the big hound would make him run for the stairs without Amy, no matter what Fergus did.

Fergus took two paces toward the staircase.

The robber's nerve broke, and he backed up a pace. Then he shoved Amy toward Ian and bolted for the steps.

Lara grabbed at his arm as Ian caught Amy. Her grip slipped off, but it was enough to make the man lose his balance at the top of the stairs. With a cry, he tumbled down them and landed spread-eagled and groaning. Then his head lolled to the side, and he went silent.

"Is he dead?" Amy asked, her voice breathless. She hid her face against Ian's chest.

Ian hugged her. "I don't think so," he told her and handed her off to her mother. He descended to the robber, knelt and checked his wrist for a pulse. "He's alive. Out cold. Lara, call the constable, if ye will." He pulled his mobile from his back pocket as he climbed back up the steps, and handed it to her. "Fergus and I will keep an eye on that...gentleman...until help gets here."

Fergus disappeared.

When Ian looked down the steps, he was already sitting by the robber. "That's a neat trick," Ian muttered. At the bottom of the steps, Ian stripped off the man's ski mask and swore. Jimmy Barth, one of Rollo's subcontractors. He must have overheard one of them talking about what was up here. Or come up himself when Caitlin and Lara were elsewhere. Well, he wouldn't be a problem any longer. While Lara talked to the constable on the mobile, Ian stripped the man's belt and used it to lash his hands together. Then he glanced from Fergus, who waited patiently, his attention on their prisoner, to the wide-eyed twins peering down from the top of the staircase.

"How did you know his name is Fergus?" Ian asked, hoping to distract them from the man on the floor.

Alex shrugged. "We saw his picture."

"I'll take that as an admission of guilt you've been somewhere you were told not to go," Ian teased, rocking back on his heels. Relief was starting to flood him. Everyone was safe. And the ghost, Fergus, had protected the twins as well as the treasures of the hidden room from the man in front of them.

Lara finished her call, frowned at Fergus, and shook her head, then turned her frown on her children. "What were you doing up here after you were supposed to be in bed?"

"It's Halloween. We hadn't looked for Fergus, yet," Amy said. "Everyone said this was the best night to find him."

"You didn't need to find him," Lara responded. "You saw him when we got home, didn't you?"

Alex nodded. "We wanted to see where he lived."

"Of course," Ian interjected, unable to miss the tension in Lara's jaw. "And we were too busy talking in the library to help."

"Exactly," Alex answered.

In a stage whisper, Amy told Ian, "I whispered to him to

find you," then continued in her normal, but shaky voice, "while Alex was talking to that man."

"That was smart, Amy," Ian told her.

Lara rolled her eyes, then gestured at the hound. "How are we going to explain him?"

Ian grinned at Lara and shrugged. "I say we don't try. Barth thought he was real. If the constable sees him, maybe he will, too. If he doesn't see him, nothing will seem strange." Then he turned to their resident ghost. "This has to be the most excitement you've seen in a couple of centuries," Ian told Fergus.

Amy giggled.

Fergus wagged his tail, then returned to keeping an eye on their prisoner, who opened his eyes, took one look at the hound looming over him, and squeezed them shut again.

~

*L*ara's hands shook, so she hid them behind her back. She'd just watched a ghost guard her children and intimidate a burglar. What would have happened if the ironmonger's tale had been the right one instead of what Ian and Caitlin had guessed about Fergus? She could barely wrap her mind around what happened here tonight, much less imagine a large, armed ghost clanking around in chain mail and wielding a giant sword. The burglar would have died of heart failure, and so would she. No, if they had to have a ghost, Fergus was a much better version, and certainly more kid-friendly.

Fortunately, when the constable arrived to take custody of the burglar, Fergus made himself scarce.

"He's going with me," the constable told them as he put cuffs on their prisoner, "but one of you will have to come down and file a complaint for unlawful entry, attempted theft…"

"And threatening my children!" Lara interjected, laying a hand on their shoulders. Alex and Amy looked tired. Now that the excitement was almost over, the adrenaline rush was fading. She needed to get them to bed soon. If they stood here much longer, she and Ian would have to carry them back to their rooms.

"What about that beast of theirs, threatening me," the burglar complained as the constable hauled him to his feet.

Amy snorted but didn't say anything. Alex just grinned.

Lara traded a relieved glance with Ian. The burglar seemed to have thought Fergus was real, so they didn't have to scramble to discredit his ravings about a ghost hound. One small mercy in a crazy night.

"He never touched you," Ian answered.

"If you're scared of dogs, that's your problem," Alex taunted.

Lara squeezed Alex's shoulder, warning him to keep quiet.

The constable prodded his charge forward. "Afraid of a wee pup, are you?"

"'Tweren't no wee pup. It was a deerhound. A big one." The man tried to spread his hands, but the cuffs stopped him. Then he tilted his head toward Ian. "He said he'd let it pull me down and do what it does to a deer!"

"Well, I don't see any blood," the constable chided, "so let's get you out of here." He nodded to Lara. "Enjoy the rest of your evening, ma'am. Kids, the excitement is over. Sleep tight." He turned to Ian. "I'll see you later, Baron."

Lara choked back a gasp. She thought she'd been through as much as anyone could stand in one night. Then the constable called Ian Baron. She suddenly and heartily wished she'd let Ian talk earlier this evening. As much as she'd enjoyed what they'd done before the kids yelled and Fergus appeared out of nowhere, this was the final straw. If even the constable called Ian Baron, she must be the only person in town who didn't. What did everyone know that she didn't?

Ian colored, then nodded. "I'll walk you out."

"No need. I'll let you wrap things up here."

After the constable took his prisoner away, Lara herded the twins and Ian down to the kitchen. First things first, she told herself, setting aside her irritation. She put a hand on Ian's arm. "You must be hurt," she told him. "That man landed a few punches…"

"I'm fine."

Ian's flat tone warned her off. She sucked in a breath, determined to make him see reason. "You're going to have bruises, if you don't already, and maybe a cracked rib, or worse. Let me look…"

The twins were watching the adults, wide-eyed and no doubt listening carefully to every word.

"Really, I'm okay." He gave her a tired smile. "You need to stay with the twins. I'll go back to the village to file the report," he offered. "It's on the way to my flat."

Lara nodded. He was right, but she was still worried. "Only if you're sure you're okay."

"Of course he is, Mom," Alex piped up. "That guy didn't stand a chance against Ian."

Ian grinned at Alex, then gazed at Lara with a lifted eyebrow. "I'll help you get the twins settled before I go. That should give you time to stop worrying about me."

"That's probably not long enough," Amy interjected. "She's a world-class worrier."

"That's not true," Lara objected. "And if I worry, it's because I care about you two."

"What about Ian?" Amy smirked. "If you're worried about him, you must care about him, too."

Lara closed her eyes. Out of the mouths of babes? Really? "I care about anybody who's hurt, silly," she said, tap-dancing for all she was worth. She didn't dare look at Ian.

"Come on, kids. Everyone is tired. Let's get you to bed."

The sudden sound of his voice startled her into a quick glance his way. The rat! He was grinning at her. But when the kids moved to obey, she sighed and nodded her thanks.

Twenty minutes later, Ian wished the twins good night. "Ye needn't fash," he told them. "Fergus will keep watch over the house. Sweet dreams." He closed their doors.

Lara wanted to fold herself into his arms and forget about the burglar and the constable calling him Baron, if only for a few minutes.

But Ian held a finger up to his lips, then pointed down the stairs and gestured for her to precede him. In the foyer, he kept his voice low. "I'll go now," he said and reached for the doorknob.

"Wait, Ian, we need to talk. You wanted to tell me something…"

"No' tonight lass. I've still got to do the report." He opened the door, letting in cold air—or was Fergus nearby? If so, he didn't show himself. Instead, Ian stepped out with a quiet, "Good night," then closed the door behind him.

Lara couldn't believe it. She leaned her forehead against the door, the events of the evening running through her mind like a movie on fast-forward. The images stalled when she got to the last few minutes. Ian reassuring the twins, wishing them sweet dreams.

She didn't know whether to be sad or angry that he hadn't done the same for her. Instead, Ian left without giving her a promise of when they would talk…or a goodnight kiss.

CHAPTER 11

$\mathcal{L}$ara had never been to Ian's office in the village. She debated going right after she dropped the twins at school, but her nerve failed her. Instead, she ducked into the tea shop for a pot of mildly caffeinated courage and a scone.

She'd heard enough bits and pieces from Caitlin, Becky, Blane and Cassie, Rollo, even the constable, for God's sake, and from Ian himself, to make her certain there was more to the nickname Baron than she knew. The obvious interpretation worried her. Barons were minor nobility, after all, even in Scotland, but why would Ian be reluctant to tell her he had a title?

She'd always wondered why Angus had decided against hiring a general contractor to help him with such a big job. He knew what he was doing, but someone to help manage the project would have saved him a lot of time and stress—and maybe his life, damn it, especially someone so obviously qualified as Ian. She'd re-read the paperwork Angus saved, but hadn't found any answers.

Nothing Ian had said or done made her doubt the quality of his work or his dedication to finishing the restoration. Or his care and concern for her and the twins. Or how he wanted her. She had felt the very large and rock-hard proof of his desire for her last night.

She just had a pervading sense that something important had been withheld, something he'd finally been ready to tell her last night. And that omission set her teeth on edge. After what she'd seen—Fergus guarding the twins until she and Ian arrived and helping Ian subdue the robber—she was fairly certain the ghost, who was supposed to obey the laird, had given the secret away. Baron. Laird. What difference did a title make? If Ian was the laird the legend said the ghost obeyed, he had more to do with Cairn Dubh than restoring it. Much more.

Fortified by her morning tea and growing irritation, Lara decided she could finally confront Ian and get some answers.

She showed up unannounced at Ian's office mid-morning. The building looked like many of its neighbors—old, well-kept, even genteel. She entered into a waiting area as chic and modern as the building housing the office was not. She could see how the contrast would appeal to Ian, even if it jarred her a bit at first. His receptionist was brisk and off-putting when Lara admitted she had no appointment. Lara convinced her to let Ian know she was there. After a quick intercom call, she smiled and ushered Lara down a short hall to Ian's private office.

There, Lara got another surprise. It might have been called an office, but it looked like a cross between a draftsman's workshop and an art studio. Oversized blueprints and sketches, including some beautiful pen & inks of Cairn Dubh, were tacked to three walls under high windows that let in the uncertain Scottish sunlight. A tilted drafting table, a desk piled high with paperwork that nearly hid the computer screen atop it, and a small seating area took up most of the floor space. Framed certificates, photos and other memorabilia filled the fourth wall behind the desk.

"Thanks, Lenore," Ian said to the receptionist, who quickly closed the door, leaving them alone. He let Lara finish her inspection before he approached her. Then he took her hand and turned the full force of his gaze on her.

The same gaze he'd used last night to make her reckless with wanting him. Lara's knees went weak. What was she doing here? This was Ian's place. His business. His stronghold. Last night he'd proven she was nearly powerless against him—or against her need for him. Then he'd left her suddenly, with barely a word and without a kiss. No way would she get him sufficiently off-balance in here to admit anything he'd held back these last weeks.

Coming to his office was a mistake. He'd been willing to talk last night and she hadn't let him. What right did she have to demand answers now? She should have waited until he came out to the house and was ready to have this conversation.

"This is a welcome surprise," he told her, his tone warm, but his expression quizzical. "Is there a problem at Cairn

Dubh? Rollo hasn't called. Or is Fergus bothering Caitlin?" he added with an altogether too adorable grin.

She wasn't sure what reception she expected, but Ian acting like nothing had happened when he left was not it. Lara shook her head and found her voice. "No, no problem. Not there." Her nerve was failing her, and she had to get it back. She straightened.

The grin disappeared. "Which implies you have one elsewhere. Here," he added, giving her an assessing stare. "So this is about last night?"

What did he expect after she showed up here for the first time ever? "Yes." She took a breath and plunged ahead. "After last night, I realized how little I really know about you, given where our evening almost went." She cleared her throat, somewhat embarrassed by bringing her attempt at seduction into the conversation. "It's time you told me more about yourself. More than I see here," she added, gesturing at the wall of certificates. "And all of what you started to say last night. What you've been hiding from me."

Ian didn't comment. He left her long enough to clear a stack of books from an upholstered chair, then ushered her to it and took a seat opposite her.

His brow slightly crinkled. He looked so endearing, she wanted to reach out, cup his cheek, and reassure him. But no, she was the one who needed reassurance, and she'd come here to get it. She fought to get her thoughts in order, or as much in order as she could when facing Ian. Her gut was telling her now wasn't the time. She'd caught him off guard, and he was going to stall some more, tell her this wasn't the place to have the conversation. In his office. During his workday.

Why hadn't she gone straight home instead of coming here?

"I should apologize," he told her. "I've wanted to tell ye long before now, but—"

"We've become friends, haven't we?" She kicked herself for stopping him, and worse, for changing the subject. But given his hesitancy, a softer tone might draw the truth out of him.

"We have. That and more," he added, his frown deepening. "At least I think so. It seemed so last night."

Until he left. Her heart suddenly pounded at his implication. This wasn't going to be easy, but she was determined to gain control of this conversation. "Friends tell each other the truth."

"Usually." Ian looked decidedly concerned now, his brows drawn together into a frown. "Lara, I—"

"But you've been keeping something from me for weeks. Perhaps as long as I've known you. I think it has something to do with why Angus didn't hire you."

Ian didn't move, but he colored and a muscle in his jaw jumped. "Why would ye think that?"

Lara was perversely pleased to hear his accent suddenly thicken, a sure sign of his discomfort.

"Because it also has something to do with why our resident ghost obeyed you…and not me."

Ian gave her a wan smile. "Halloween turned out to be—"

"Terrifying. And…illuminating." She felt torn. His

purple knuckles told her he hadn't come out of the fight entirely unscathed. She owed him for the risk he'd taken for her and the twins. "I'm so grateful you were there to protect the twins—with a little help from Fergus—and to stop that man." But he owed her answers. "Don't you think we've been through enough together for you to come clean? How bad can it be?"

Ian blew out a breath and leaned back. "Bad enough ye'll want nay more to do with me. And to find someone else to finish the restoration."

That accent. Lara's chest suddenly hollowed out. "What? You can't be serious."

"Ye heard me, lass." He crossed his arms.

She gripped her chair. "It's why people call you Baron when they think I can't hear, isn't it?"

Ian stood and walked to a window. With his back to her, he stared silently out while his shoulders lifted and fell. "I tried to tell you last night, before we…got carried away. And then we were interrupted." He turned suddenly to face her. "This morning, I…this is not how I wanted to tell you. I don't want to hurt you, Lara. I never did." He raked a hand through his hair. "What I haven't told you will hurt. You'll draw the wrong conclusion."

"You can't know that."

"Trust me, I do. I thought about this a lot last night."

He paused again and Lara held her breath. After filling out the police complaint, he must have been awake the rest of the night. He looked tired. Defeated, and hardly the hero he'd been for her and her twins' last night.

"It's better for both of us if I leave things as they are," he finally said. "Better if you don't see me again."

Lara's heart dropped and she sucked in a breath while Ian's gaze moved away from her, toward the wall of certificates behind his desk. None of this made any sense.

"I'll have my accountant draw up a bill for the plans and the work done so far," he told the wall, then turned his gaze back to her. "Caitlin will, as well. Another firm, and another appraiser, can complete the rest of the work. I already asked the constable to keep a patrol near the estate —or on it—to deter further treasure-hunters. I've done all I can do for you…Mrs. MacLaren. I'm sorry."

What? Suddenly, he returned to calling her Mrs. MacLaren? "Damn it, Ian, no." She leaned toward him. "I don't want anyone else. You have some sort of… connection…to Cairn Dubh. I've seen how much you care about it."

Ian grimaced. "That doesn't matter."

"It does. I think it's the key to all of this…this mystery. The secret you've been keeping. Besides…there is no one else."

"There will be. Once I'm out of the way, you'll receive plenty of bids. Good, reasonable bids."

"No one would take the job but you."

"Because I told them not to."

"What? You kept others from bidding on the job? You're scaring me, you know." She fought for something to say to ease the tension. "Are you some sort of Scottish mafia don?" That seemed to help. One corner of his lip quirked up, but as quickly pulled back down.

"There is no such thing."

"I didn't think there was." She spread her hands, palms up. "So what is this about? Are you angry with me? After last night, have the twins gotten to be too much of a complication? Or are you just determined to keep me in the dark? Whatever it is, I can take it. We can deal with it."

Ian shook his head. "I ken what this will do to ye, and I never meant to hurt ye." He walked to the door and opened it. "Go home, Lara, and make some calls."

Lara tried to stand, but her legs wouldn't support her, and she landed back on her fanny in the chair. She'd never foreseen challenging Ian resulting in this. Why hadn't she gone home? He'd suddenly become a cold, distant stranger, as if they'd never met and the past months had never happened. As if last night had never happened.

Whatever he was hiding had to be huge to make him this defensive. She looked around the office, then forced herself to her feet, went to the wall of certificates and studied them. She could feel Ian's scowl boring into her back, but she ignored him. Unless he picked her up and carried her out, she wasn't leaving his office. Not yet. Not until she figured something out.

She read every official-looking document, even puzzling her way through some Latin inscriptions, thanks to a year of study in high school she'd always thought a waste of time—until now. She found nothing. Not a clue in the lot.

"It's a bit late to be so interested in my qualifications," Ian intoned behind her.

Refusing to admit defeat, Lara gave him the same hard

stare she used on the twins. "You might as well tell me. You started to last night, so tell me now. I won't give up asking. You know I won't." She waited for a response, arms crossed and jaw clenched.

Ian just watched her, like a mouse watching a cat.

She threw her hands out wide. "Would you rather I hear it from someone else?" she demanded, at wit's end. "Someone in this town will eventually slip up and tell me what's going on. If not you or Caitlin, then Rollo or Becky or…"

He closed the door. It felt like a victory, albeit a small one. Lara wanted to cheer, but had a strong sense Ian wasn't going to give her anything to cheer about.

"Sit down," he told her. Not an invitation this time.

She stood her ground and gave him her most intimidating stare, daring him to try to make her.

He studied her for another long minute, then spoke. "I should have told you right away. But I think your late husband turned me down because of what I have to tell you."

Not again! Lara's belly clenched. "I knew he had something to do with this!"

Ian shook his head. "Nay, he didna. But losing the job was a blow. There was so much I needed to learn."

"About Cairn Dubh."

"Aye. At first." He crossed his arms. "Then about ye and the bairns. Ye gave me the second chance I wanted. Ye became…I looked forward to seeing ye, every day. I was miserable on the days I had nay reason to go out there."

There was that accent again.

"I'm glad," she told him, forcing as much warmth into her voice as she could, even though her throat tightened and her hands shook. "Not that you were miserable. That you wanted to be with us. I wanted you there, too. I still do." She fought not to reach out to him, or to clench her hands into fists at her sides.

"I dinna ken...I don't know," he amended with a sigh, "how to tell ye, so I'll just say it." He spread his hands. "People call me Baron because 'tis said an ancestor of mine was the last Baron Macaulay in the local branch of the family. If the title still existed, and if the story is true, it would be mine. My grandda was certain Cairn Dubh is my ancestral home."

Her belly turned over. His? "Paterson..."

"A sept of the clan and a name taken by the Culloden survivors from this area. Jacobites, all, and from what I've seen, some of the things we found in the hidden rooms likely will confirm the connection."

She moved to the chair and sat, suddenly light-headed.

Ian continued talking. "Someone sealed up those rooms to protect the clan's heritage. My heritage," he added, tapping his chest. "They spread the rumor that wing of the house wasn't safe. Rollo is probably right. I imagine they buried poor Fergus at the threshold hoping the threat of his ghost would keep thieves and others out. I'm sure they expected to come back one day, but never got the chance. After Culloden, so many suspected Jacobites were hunted down and killed...or at best, exiled."

Lara's hand lifted to her throat. "That's horrible. I'm so sorry. But that means...all the contents, the whole estate, belongs to you." All Angus's dreams, all the work they'd done, and it never really belong to them?

"Nay, it all belongs to you. Legally. I have no claim on it. None at all."

She shook her head, confused. "But the legend says the ghost obeys the laird. Fergus obeyed you, not me."

"Ye noticed that."

His tone was flat. Was he so sorry she had noticed? "I did." Lara crossed her arms. "I didn't realize it at the time, but when he popped into the library, he came to you. And later, when I told him to guard the twins, not the sack the robber dropped, he looked to you. You told him to go to the stairs, and he did."

"Well, the village government is not as agreeable as the ghost. It doesn't obey the laird."

She ignored his attempt at humor. No wonder Ian was so reluctant to tell her much about himself. She hated doubting him, but several things crossed her mind all at once.

Had the invitation to Blane and Cassie's wedding truly come from them? Or had Ian arranged it to get under her skin, knowing how emotionally fraught a wedding could be? Up to that point, their relationship had been strictly business. Well, not strictly. She'd started to develop feelings for him, and had begun to imagine him doing the same.

And the time with the twins…was what he'd told her about his past, his connection to them, a lie, too? Dreading his answer to the next logical question, but needing to know, she took a breath. "So your interest in me—all of what happened in the library last night—was meant to seduce me into what? Marrying you so you could regain the rights to your heritage?" She'd been a fool.

"Nay, of course not." Ian clenched his fists. "I care…but, it's not like that. My interest in you has nothing to do with Cairn Dubh."

Who was he kidding? She curled her fingers into her palms, mirroring his action, his tension. Heart breaking, she told him, "It seems very much like that to me."

Ian spread his hands. "I told you that you would draw the wrong conclusion."

Lara stiffened, dismay and anger making her throat tight, her voice loud. "What other conclusion do you expect me to draw? You have a stake in the estate I own, in the things we found in the hidden rooms, their history if not their value. In the States, we call what you've been doing a long con." She gripped the arms of her chair. She'd been through this with Angus when, after an argument, he claimed he'd married her for her money. They'd gotten past the hurt that caused and learned to love each other for the twins' sake, and their own, but she refused to be used like that a second time.

Ian didn't say a word. Maybe his jaw was too tight to let him speak. His expression looked frozen, the skin over his cheekbones stiff and pale, his lips compressed so far as to be almost invisible.

She'd always believed he'd been honest with her.

The hollow in her gut told her she'd been wrong.

Lara stood. This time her knees supported her. Her backbone rigid, she crossed the office to the door and put her hand on the knob.

"Rollo can remove any equipment you have left on site," she said to the doorframe. "I don't want you to upset the twins, so don't go out there again." Heart pounding hard enough to break, she opened the door and stepped through into the hallway without looking back.

Ian made no move to stop her.

She kept her eyes focused straight ahead, ignoring Ian's receptionist's cheery farewell as she passed her desk. She couldn't think about how to fire Caitlin. How to find a new general contractor or a new appraiser didn't even enter into the misery she felt. Walking away from Ian felt like losing everything. How could she break this news to the twins who'd lost their father and were about to lose the man they'd come to love in his place?

She got into her car and sat, keys in hand, fingers numb. Snow had started to fall while Ian turned her world upside down. It covered her windshield in a lacy blanket of white, hiding her from passersby. As alone as she could be in the middle of town, she let her tears fall, too.

~

It took all the restraint Ian possessed not to go after her, to beg her to forgive him, to get down on his knees and promise anything she wanted. But Ian managed to close his office door quietly. Then he collapsed into the seat Lara vacated moments before, rubbing a hand over his sore midsection. By now, he expected some colorful bruises would be showing up, but he was fairly certain the robber hadn't broken any ribs with the punches he'd landed. Lara would feel terrible about that. Or she would have, before he'd confessed.

Shite! He scrubbed both hands over his face then pounded a fist on the arm of the chair. What had he done? Could telling Lara the truth have gone any worse? She'd fought for a few minutes to get him to open up. He'd been glad of that, hoping it meant she'd listen and understand why he'd delayed telling her. Then he'd confessed what he'd been hiding. After that, even after she said she cared, he'd been unable to make her understand why he'd hidden the truth, and why the only way he could think to prove he wanted her was to walk away. But she'd been the one to walk away. Ian feared he'd never get her back. Her face had drawn tight, white lines appearing around the thin slash of her lips just before she strode, ramrod straight, to the door and told him she didn't even want him to pick up his equipment.

I don't want you to upset the twins.

He didn't want to upset them, either. Or their mother. But it was too late. Bollocks! Couldn't she see what she and the twins meant to him? Instead, she'd turned to ice and marched out, furious and feeling betrayed because she thought the reason for his interest in her, and his attempts to seduce her, had meant nothing to him but a way to take control of Cairn Dubh. Exactly as he'd expected. Couldn't she understand he was trying to protect her, not to hurt her?

But he had hurt her. That was obvious. Quitting the restoration like this had seemed the only way to prove he wanted her for herself, not for what she owned. It wasn't professional, and he was certain it felt personal to Lara.

What else could he do? He got up and started pacing, from the door to the windows and back again.

She knew the truth now. And she'd walked out as cold and silent as the falling snow he could see through his office windows. She'd reacted exactly as he'd feared, assuming he only wanted to take advantage of her.

He'd get the paperwork drawn up to break the contract. And that would be that.

Except it wouldn't. He couldn't let Lara go. He had to find a way to win her back.

Ian's intercom buzzed. Startled out of his brooding, he froze in his tracks, then went to the desk to answer it. "Yes, Lenore?" The steady sound of his voice surprised him.

"It's Caitlin."

"Thanks, I've got it." He didn't want to talk to anyone, but punched the button for the outside line anyway. "Caitlin?"

"I found the proof, Ian. Jacobites, as we expected. Several things with dates, the Macaulay plaid, swords with cranberries etched into the blades. And gold coins! Wait till you see!"

His heart plummeted into his belly and he sank into the chair behind his desk. "I may never get to. Lara was just here, demanding answers. I told her everything. She reacted...well, it wasn't good. In fact, it was exactly what I expected. So I'm breaking the contract."

"Have ye lost yer mind?" Caitlin's screech made Ian hold the phone away from his ear.

"And my hearing. Wheesht!"

"Ye bloody arse. Get over here and take it all back. Crawl if ye must. The answers are here, and I canna continue this research without her permission. If ye've angered her, broken her trust, ye must come here and fix it."

Ian sighed. "She won't listen."

"Ye must make her listen!"

"She told me not to darken her door—"

"She's not thinking straight. You surprised her...damn it, I warned you about this. Once she has a chance to think it over, she'll realize you really care for her and the twins—"

"It won't matter. She'll never trust me again. You were right, I should have told her weeks ago."

"Baron, this is too important for you to wallow in hurt feelings, or her, either."

"Important to whom, Caitlin? To Lara? Not at all. To you and me? Aye. To posterity? Well, that's up to Lara now."

"Not if you reason with her."

"When she left here, she was in no mood to reason."

"Then give her a chance to breathe, and some time to think, then come over and kiss her senseless. My God, cousin. We've got more family history in our hands than anyone has seen in over two hundred years. You can't just let that go."

Ian's temper flared and he snapped, "Aye, I can. And I have."

"*Eedjit!*" Caitlin exclaimed and cut the connection.

Ian hung up the phone and dropped his head into his hands. Caitlin was right. He was an idiot. He'd lost his mind. He'd wonder where his sanity had fled to, but he knew the answer. To Cairn Dubh, in the arms of a certain bright-eyed lass with two irresistible twins and the ghost of a prized Scottish deerhound.

Who obeyed him. Acknowledged him as its laird.

Fergus had convinced Lara that he had a right to be there. When he'd admitted he might have more of a claim than a mere ghost's acknowledgement, he'd frightened her more than Fergus had. She thought everything they'd shared had been a lie.

If only he'd told her the truth up front. He'd dug himself quite a hole—deeper than the one where Fergus lay. Now he had to figure out how to climb out of it, win the woman he loved, and if there was an honorable way to do it, claim his heritage. Or give it up forever. The only thing that mattered was Lara.

He lifted his head and stared out the window at the snowflakes drifting by. His jaw dropped. The woman he loved...his heart did a little somersault in his chest. Aye, he did.

He'd never told her.

Before he knew it, he was on his feet. The answer couldn't be that simple. But it was a place to start—if she'd listen to him for just five minutes. Caitlin was right about this, too. He'd crawl if he had to. He'd do whatever Lara wanted, whatever it took to convince her he meant it when he said he wanted to be with her. He wanted her. Angus's decision had denied him the chance to run Cairn Dubh's restoration and learn what he could from it. He'd accepted that, until Lara had given him a second chance. He still wanted that chance, but he wanted Lara and the twins more. All the rest was a bonus. Generations had lived without the answers held in that estate. He could, too.

~

Lara couldn't believe the nerve of the man. She'd just gotten home from driving aimlessly around in the snow, all the while nursing her sense of betrayal into something monumental, and wondering what to do next and how to tell the twins, when someone knocked on the door. She answered it, only to find Ian standing on the front portico.

"I thought I told you not to come here again."

"I was hoping we could talk some more before ye have to fetch the twins. I—"

"I think you said quite enough already."

"I love you, Lara. I never told you, and I should have."

Heart threatening to burst, she gripped the edge of the door. The urge to slam it in his face receded as she stepped back and fought to process what Ian had just revealed. "You do not. You're just trying to get control of what we found here."

"That was…unexpected." He looked away for a long moment. "Hoped for, but unexpected." Then he dropped to his knees before her.

Lara swallowed her shock and stared down at him, still poised to shut him out.

"Ye were even more unexpected. More than I ever dared hope for. Ye do no' have to marry me," he told her, his voice deep, his accent thick, and his tone sincere. "No' ever. This place does no' ever have to be mine. The only thing I canna live without is ye. Alex and Amy, too. Wherever ye go, I'll go with ye. Back to California, if that is what ye wish. It does no' matter to me where I am, as long as I'm with ye."

She could not have heard him correctly. "You would leave here? Leave all this?" She waved at the scene behind him, Scotland in snow, so beautiful.

"To be with ye? Aye."

Lara didn't know what to say. She needed time to think. "Ian…get up, for God's sake. I just got home from driving around, talking myself into hating you." She reached for his hand and hauled him to his feet, suddenly awash in dismay when her hand chilled from contact with his. Hers went cold any time her emotions got too strong. He hadn't been out in the snow very long. He must be overwrought. His chilled skin convinced her, as much as any of his words, his emotions were fully involved, and he meant what he said. "Come inside. If you stay in front of the door there much longer, you're going to look like a short snowman the twins built."

"If this is the only place you'll listen to me, I don't mind," he insisted and bent his knees, prepared to drop onto them again.

"Yes, you do. Besides, we already have one ghost. Fergus doesn't need you for company in the netherworld."

Ian straightened and brushed the snow from his shoulders and out of his hair. "Thank you."

Relief eased a weight she hadn't realized she was carrying when he followed her inside and closed the door. "If you'll lay a fire in the library," she told him, "I'll make tea and we can talk." Tea would ease the chill in both of them.

"Whisky?"

"You know where it is." And a wee dram, as the Scots said, would warm them, too, and maybe melt some of the ice that had formed between them today.

By the time she got the tea ready, she had regained her equilibrium. Ian had a cheerful blaze going in the library hearth and two short drams of whisky on the side table. To her surprise, Fergus stretched his translucent length across the hearthstones in front of the fire. Ian shrugged when she glanced his way and gave her a slight shake of his head. So he hadn't summoned the hound—if he could. Did Fergus know what they were going to discuss? What was at stake for both of them? All of them, she amended. The twins, too. Even Fergus, she supposed. He'd waited a long, long time for a laird to return to Cairn Dubh. Maybe Ian wasn't the laird he knew, who'd prized Fergus enough to have that painting done, and who'd left him behind to guard his keep. But Fergus didn't seem to mind.

She set the tea tray on the whisky table and poured for both of them into mugs, American style. She'd still been sulking, she supposed, in the kitchen. Now, she needed to do her level best to ignore the ghostly presence. She was pleased to see her hands didn't shake. She wouldn't say she was accustomed to Fergus, but after Halloween night, she'd accepted him. He'd alerted them, held the robber at bay, and protected the twins until she and Ian could get to them. She wondered if one could be grateful to a ghost. And would the ghost sense it?

She took a seat on the opposite end of the couch from Ian. They sipped their tea silently. Fergus appeared to be asleep in front of the fire. Did ghosts sleep? There was so much she didn't know. About everything. Maybe she should go home, back to where things were familiar.

"Perhaps it would be best if the twins and I returned to California."

Ian sloshed some tea over the back of his hand and swore.

Fergus opened one eye, then stood and took a step toward Ian.

Lara held her breath. What would Fergus do?

"I'm all right, laddie," Ian assured the ghost, setting his mug aside and wiping the back of his hand with the other, then pursing his lips and blowing across it to cool it.

Fergus sat, watching Ian for a moment as if making sure he was really okay, then returned to the hearth and stretched out.

Lara shook her head. The ghost had shown concern for its laird? What next? She couldn't believe she could be so calm about his presence, much less that he would interact with one of them. But then, Ian was the laird he'd waited for all these years.

"Why?" Ian asked.

His question pulled her attention back to him. For a crazy moment, she thought he was still speaking to Fergus and wondered how the ghost would reply. She struggled to recall what she'd said to elicit his question. Oh yes, going back to California. Ian pursed his lips and blew across the back of his hand again while she'd ruminated, and she recalled the last time those lips had been on her. She loved Ian's kiss, his touch. He'd awakened feelings she'd thought gone forever with Angus. But loving Ian would be complicated. She nodded at the apparition on the hearthstones. "Him, for one. I'll sell Cairn Dubh to you."

"You know I can't afford it, or I would have bought it before now." Ian's tone was dry as dust.

She realized she'd just forced him to declare something no man wanted to admit. "Then I'll give it to you. The gold we found should be more than enough to take care of taxes and let you keep it."

Ian went so still she feared Fergus would react as if he was in danger. Fergus did raise his head and stare at Ian, then her, then back at Ian, but he settled down again.

Lara released a breath.

So did Ian. "You can't afford to do that. And the gold belongs in a museum. Or a trust. Or something. Even with it, I still wouldn't afford the taxes and upkeep, over time. My business is successful, but not to that level."

So much for the vaunted male ego.

His honesty cheered her. Painful though it had been, they'd had a breakthrough at his office. Despite their defensiveness, walls had come down between them. They'd both admitted their feelings for the other, though Ian had done his best to shield her from his. To make her think he didn't care. Which, once she thought about it, told her he did care, a lot. In his office, at that point, she hadn't been able to deal with the rawness of the wound he'd inflicted on her, or the extent of the lie he'd been living the whole time he'd been with her. She'd walked out, and she regretted doing that. But she'd had time to calm down and think about everything Ian told her, and how he'd said it. She just wasn't quite ready to let him know yet.

"So if the twins and I go back to California, you'd really come with us? Give up everything you have here? Your business? Your friends and family? Cairn Dubh and its ghost?" She shook her head. "I don't believe you."

"'Twould no' be an easy thing to do, but I would. Ye mean too much to me, Lara. Nothing here has ever made me as happy as being with ye and the twins."

His thickened accent told her he was feeling the strain—and letting her know it. She owed him the same courtesy he'd finally shown her—her honesty for his.

"I don't want to go back to California," she admitted. After setting her mug aside, she reached for the whisky and handed a glass to Ian. "I don't want to give up Cairn Dubh to anyone but you."

Ian watched her like a cornered hound, wary and yet, at the same time hopeful.

"I hear a 'but' coming…"

Lara sipped the spirit, swallowed, and coughed. Ian waited while she got her heart and her throat under control. It was time to lay her cards on the table. "No, you don't. I won't give Cairn Dubh to anyone else." She set her glass aside and faced him. "I don't want to lose you, Ian. I want you here, with me. In any way you can accept."

Under his furrowed brow, Ian's eyes were wide. "I want that, too."

"You know you get more than me in the deal."

"I ken it. I love the twins."

He loved the twins, and yet he'd never told her he loved her until today.

"I love ye, too. I want to spend all of my life with ye, Lara, but only if you wish to. I won't have you think I'm trying to take anything from you. I'm not. I'll sign anything ye wish, give up any claim, past or future." He set his glass aside and leaned toward her, held out his hand, then pulled it back and clenched it, as if he'd thought better of reaching for her. "There's so much I want to give you. And the twins. I can't compete with your wealth, but I can—I do—love all of you."

"They'll be teenagers in a few years," she warned him.

"We'll deal with them…together."

That warmed her more than the fire Ian built for them. "You've already got them under your spell."

"What about their mother? Is she under my spell, as well?"

Lara sighed and gave him the first smile she'd managed since they'd argued in his office. "Yes. I am."

Ian got off the couch, knelt before her, and took her hands in his.

"You've really got to stop doing that," she told him with a nervous laugh.

"I love you, Lara. What can I say or do to make you believe me? I want to wake up with you each morning and go to bed with you each night. I want to help you raise the twins. I want to be a father to them. I ken I canna replace Angus, but I want to be the best father I can for them."

"You're a brave man, Ian Paterson...or should I say Macaulay?"

"Paterson will do," he told her and lifted her hands to his mouth. He dropped kisses on the back, making fire race up her arms to her heart. "Will ye have me, lass? Anyway ye wish."

His dark hair gleamed ruddy in the firelight. Over his shoulder, Lara caught Fergus watching them with wide, dark eyes. Ian had protected the twins. She couldn't ask for more proof he cared about them—even loved them. He'd faced a robber and a ghost, all at once. He'd be a good father to them, and to any other children they might have.

She met Ian's soulful gaze. In this light, his eyes were as dark as Fergus's, wide with anxiety...and hope. He offered her a future she never would have anticipated when she and Angus moved here. *Oh, Angus, if only you could know I'm not alone anymore...and that we're loved.* Her glance strayed to Fergus for a moment. *And protected. You just wouldn't believe how.* She lifted a hand to Ian's cheek and trailed her fingers down it, then smiled as he caught her hand and kissed her fingertips, never taking his gaze from hers. She was ready for the future and everything it would bring.

"Marry me, Ian. I love you and I want to spend the rest of my life with you."

"Ach, Lara, do ye mean it?" he murmured, eyes blazing. Then he leaned forward to claim her mouth in a soul-searing kiss. "I will," he finally answered. "I can't imagine my life without ye in it."

She wrapped her arms around his shoulders and pulled him off his knees and onto the couch, needing to feel his heat, his weight, his desire, with her entire body. Ian obliged, stretching out on top of her and kissing his way down her throat.

"Wait!" she called and glanced toward the fireplace, where Fergus was now standing.

Ian took her meaning. "Back to yer byre with ye, laddie. This is just between my lady and me."

Fergus disappeared.

"That's a neat trick," Lara observed, her voice breathy with need. "Now we're alone, my laird…"

"Aye, my lady. Aye!"

When she looked through the entrance to Cairn Dubh's renovated, but as yet unfurnished great hall in the old wing, Lara gasped. She'd never imagined it so full of people.

Ian had worked steadily to put in plumbing and power, and to finish the areas visitors would see on their way in, including the ground floor hallway and powder room, the main stairs and the first floor powder room and hallway leading to this grand space. He'd also finished a new master suite on the upper floor. Lara had enjoyed shopping to furnish it. The furniture had arrived last week, and the new curtains had been hung just yesterday.

Through the great hall's sparkling newly installed windows, she could see brilliant sunshine and the bright green of springtime leaves bursting from the trees, in contrast against the blue sky. He'd found an artist who could copy and extend an old wallpaper pattern she adored, so while the walls were plain white, the ceiling glinted with medieval illuminations of fanciful beasts, including the occasional deerhound, and colorful flowers picked out in gilt. Deep moldings, painted white and accented with gilt, adorned the tops of the walls and the medallions above the crystal chandeliers. They were lit and the bulbs added to the sunlight passing through them, painting rainbows on the walls.

She couldn't imagine a more colorful and magical scene.

Though the registrar would officiate today, this would by no means be the same as the small ceremony she'd attended with Ian for Blane and Cassie. More of their friends, and hundreds of people she'd yet to meet, stood to either side of the room. They formed a wide center aisle she would traverse to reach Ian, who stood at the opposite end, next to the registrar, in full, resplendent, Highland dress—deep red plaid kilt, white-furred sporan decorating the front, sgian dubh tucked in his boot, and all. Blane stood on his other side, flanked by Alex, who looked quite uncomfortably Scottish in his specially made wedding kilt in the blue MacLaren tartan.

Amy and Caitlin waited opposite the registrar, ready to stand with her. Both wore frilly white blouses. Caitlin wore a long plaid skirt matching her cousin's tartan, and Amy wore a long plaid skirt matching her brother's kilt.

Lara couldn't help noticing they gave the room a subtle but fitting touch of red, white, and blue.

Then Fergus moved out from behind Ian and sat in front of him, as if challenging her approach.

Lara's belly twisted, making her swallow. Could anyone

see him? Ian hadn't flinched and the crowd stayed calm, so Fergus must have made himself visible only to her, much as he had to the twins after Ian first opened this wing. From somewhere off to her side, a harp started playing the tune she'd chosen for her entrance. It gave her the courage to take the first step. She nearly stumbled when Fergus stood and moved to stand next to Alex, who also seemed unaware of his presence, at the end of the row of males flanking Ian. She took that to mean all this was okay with their friendly ghost. He'd merely been making sure she saw him. She gave him a quick nod of acknowledgement, then turned her attention to keeping her feet under her and her focus on Ian.

His smile drew her like the sight of Fergus drew her twins. As she neared the front of the hall, someone reached out a hand. Becky! Next to her, Cassie wore the blue scarf that had been Lara's wedding gift to her. Lara squeezed her hand and kept going. She wondered what Ian would think when he noticed the length of ancient Macaulay plaid Caitlin had found in a chest in the second floor's hidden room and draped across Lara's torso. She'd pinned it at the shoulder with a clasp shaped like a cluster of berries and told Lara she hoped the fabric would hold together long enough to get through the ceremony.

Ian's eyebrows shot up as she reached him. So he had noticed. Then he smiled and nodded, took her hand and turned to face the registrar.

She'd heard the ceremony before, thanks to Blane and Cassie. Today, though she knew the registrar was speaking, her every sense was attuned to Ian. She couldn't look anywhere else. They stood shoulder-to-shoulder, the heat from his arm warming hers. His scent filled her nose and made her long to taste his lips. His voice, deep and solemn when he answered the registrar, sent thrills of anticipation through her body, then he touched her hand and she realized the registrar had spoken to her. She said the only thing that came to mind. "I do."

Ian's smile blazed.

She got through the rest of the short ceremony in the same daze. Only Ian's kiss snapped her out of it, his warm lips melting through the fog holding her in thrall, promising so much more…later.

As Ian turned her to face their friends, she noticed Fergus, still where she'd last seen him, at Alex's left hand. She nodded to them both, then turned her head to smile at Amy and Caitlin before giving Ian a look of unconstrained joy. She didn't care who saw her. She grabbed his head and pulled him down for another melting kiss. The crowd before them broke into cheers.

"Milady!" Ian whispered against her lips.

"Yours forever," she answered the same way.

Hours later, Ian and Lara bid the last guests good night and closed the door. "We did it! Cairn Dubh's first big party in over two-hundred years," Lara exulted.

"And not to sound overly superstitious, but a good omen, I think, to start with its most important one," Ian added, pulling her into his arms.

Lara sagged against her new husband. "I don't know about you, but I'm exhausted."

Ian chuckled. "Already? The night is far from over, milady." He bent his head.

In moments, she was lost in his kiss, amazed at how quickly he could make the world go away, until there were only the two of them, wrapped in a haze of pleasure. Finally, he lifted his mouth from hers, making her moan.

"I'll get the twins settled," Ian offered. "You make some tea, and I'll meet you in the library."

Lara gave him a grateful smile. She noticed he didn't mention getting the whisky out, but they'd had plenty after the ceremony and during the reception dinner, as it seemed every guest wanted to toast their health and happiness. Yes, tea sounded perfectly…restorative. Ian had to be dead on his feet, too, but it was their wedding night, and she planned to enjoy it.

And bless her, Caitlin was spending the night in one of the guest rooms in the same wing as the twins. She would get them up and out of the house in the morning, so Lara and Ian would not be disturbed.

Lara smiled at the memory of Caitlin, when they told her about the upcoming wedding, insisting it was her right. She was going to be their 'auntie', so she was obligated to spoil them rotten. She'd repeated those words today when Lara thanked her again, and said that was exactly what she planned to do for the next week while her cousin and his new wife were away on their honeymoon. Unfortunately, both Alex and Amy had heard that declaration and had brightened up considerably. Caitlin had no idea what she was getting into. But Lara appreciated her offer, nonetheless, though she did worry about Caitlin controlling the twins in the hidden rooms by herself.

A representative from the National Museum in Edinburgh had visited last week and chosen some furniture and clan memorabilia for a display about the events following the failed Jacobite rebellion. The truck was coming to pick them up while Ian and Lara were gone. While keeping an eye on the twins, Caitlin had to finish inventorying and packing the smaller items in the next few days.

The sound of Ian's deep laughter reached her. The affection he and the twins shared warmed her right to her bones. To settle them down before bed and start their life together on the right foot, he'd planned to read them a Highland legend—and not one involving ghosts, he'd promised. No sense filling their heads with nonsense when they had a real ghost of their very own.

She hoped Ian picked a short tale to read, especially tonight. Twenty minutes later, as she brought the tea tray from the kitchen to the library, she could still hear Ian upstairs, cajoling the twins to go to sleep. Their laughter filled her heart to bursting, one more perfect touch in an already perfect day.

Lara looked forward to taking the day into a perfect night by having Ian's loving attention on her. She set the tray on the nearby whisky table, fixed her tea and sank into the overstuffed sofa in front of the fire. Mug in hand, she winked at the giant deerhound sitting in front of it.

"Aye, Fergus, ye did well today. Cairn Dubh has its laird, and at long last, so do you. And I have my wonderful new husband. I hope that doesn't mean you're going to disappear on us. We want you to stay."

Fergus stood and walked toward her.

Lara tensed for a moment, then reminded herself he'd never harmed anyone, even when he, Ian and the twins faced off against the burglar.

When he stretched out at her feet, her heart melted with the certainty he was telling her she was now his lady, as Ian was his laird. She leaned forward and tried to touch him, to let him know she understood and appreciated his gesture, but her hand met only chilled air. She drew it back and dipped her head, instead. Fergus huffed out a silent ghostly sigh and dropped his head to his paws.

Minutes later, when Ian found them like that, his eyebrows lifted, then he grinned. Without comment, he moved around Fergus's ghostly form, took Lara's mug and set it aside with his and sprawled against her on the couch. "Are you okay with him there?"

"For now. We were just waiting for you. The twins finally settled down?"

"Aye. And apparently, so has our ghostly guardian. As if we needed more proof," he told her as he leaned in for a kiss to start their evening. "All at Cairn Dubh is—finally— as it should be."

ABOUT THE AUTHOR

Willa Blair is an award-wining Amazon and Barnes & Noble #1 bestselling author of Scottish historical, light paranormal and contemporary romance, filled with men in kilts, psi talents, and plenty of spice. Her books have won numerous accolades, including the Marlene, the Merritt, National Readers' Choice Award Finalist, Booksellers' Best Award Finalist, National Excellence in Story Telling Historical Fiction Third Place Winner, Reader's Crown finalist, InD'Tale Magazine's RONE Award Honorable Mention, and NightOwl Reviews Top Picks. She loves scouting new settings for books, and thinks being an author is the best job she's ever had.

Willa loves hearing from readers!
Contact her:
www.willablair.com
authorwillablair@gmail.com

Sign up for my Newsletter
Find links to the rest of my books

www.ingramcontent.com/pod-product-compliance
Lightning Source LLC
Chambersburg PA
CBHW050327110726
47899CB00007B/2402